Danger in the Dark

"Well, I'd better get back to—" Frank's words stopped in his throat as a high scream tore through the cool mountain air from the movie set below.

Sassy Leigh, a consultant on the film, whipped her head around. "What was that?" she asked.

"Let's find out," Frank said as he and Sassy headed back down the trail.

As Frank ran along the edge of the forest, a peculiar smell drifted toward his nostrils. It was a sour, gamey, sweaty odor. Whew, Frank thought as the odor grew stronger.

He looked to his left, squinting his eyes to get a better view into the darkness of the forest. He could see lots of shadowy shapes in there, and some of them seemed to move.

It was the sudden rush toward him that caught him off guard—the huge form coming from between the trees. Frank didn't have a chance. There was no warning, no time for defense.

The Hardy Boys Mystery Stories

Available from MINSTREL Books

THE **HARDY BOYS**®

#169
GHOST OF A CHANCE

FRANKLIN W. DIXON

A MINSTREL® BOOK

Published by POCKET BOOKS
New York   London   Toronto   Sydney   Singapore

For information regarding special discounts for bulk purchases, please
contact Simon & Schuster Special Sales at 1-800-456-6798 or
business@simonandschuster.com

A MINSTREL PAPERBACK *Original*

A Minstrel Book published by
POCKET BOOKS, a division of Simon & Schuster, Inc.
1230 Avenue of the Americas, New York, NY 10020

ISBN: 0-7434-0684-2

First Minstrel Books printing September 2001

10 9 8 7 6 5 4 3 2 1

Contents

1 A Scream on the Mountain

A mist clung to the dense forest like blue-gray ghosts in the trees. The Monday morning sun hadn't quite cleared the Great Smoky Mountains. It was light, but still night-cool in the valley clearing high in an isolated area of eastern Tennessee.

Frank Hardy's brown eyes focused intently. About fifty yards ahead, a large black bear stood up on its hind legs. Its head rolled back and forth, and a rumbling roar filled the air.

As Frank watched, the bear stepped from side to side, and then dropped back down to all four paws. The animal started to run slowly toward Frank, then abruptly broke into a terrifying gallop.

The bear's furry legs revolved almost like wheels. The ground vibrated, and the pounding of the paws reminded Frank of a drumroll. The animal barreled toward Frank, but Frank didn't flinch. He stood his ground.

"Easy, Gus." Gene Posten's voice spoke up from behind Frank, who turned his head toward the man. "Slow down, boy." Gene dropped his arm and pointed to the ground. The bear slowed and finally skidded to a stop.

"Whew," Frank said, releasing his breath in one whoosh. His heart skipped with exhilaration.

"Good job, Gus," Gene said. Gus dropped back to a sitting position. "You, too, Frank," Gene added.

Gene was a tall man—Frank guessed six-four—with brown wavy hair. His leather jacket was the same shiny jet black as Gus's fur.

"Remember, bears have no interest in humans as meat," Gene said, continuing his training. "They attack to defend their territory, to protect their family, or to assert their dominance." Gene swung his arm up, and Gus leaned his head way back and made a throaty chuckling noise.

"In Gus's case, the danger is in playing. Bears like to push things for fun. In the wild, bears spend time just pushing rocks around. When Gus pushes you, you can break. So just tell him, 'No,' and sweep your arm to the right. That's his signal to stop. Now give him some treats."

Frank tossed out a handful of fish sticks, which

Gus ate with one large, sticky lapping of his thick brown tongue.

"Too bad Jumper Herman didn't have someone around to stop the bears in their tracks," Joe Hardy said, joining them. Seventeen-year-old Joe was a year younger than his brother, Frank. Gus rolled his head back and forth to welcome Joe. Joe shook his own head in a return greeting.

"Definitely," Gene's cousin Lloyd Hyser answered, patting Gus's enormous shoulder. Lloyd's hair was blond like Joe's, but straight and short.

Lloyd and Gene were both in their early thirties and owned an animal rescue farm in Tennessee. They provided a care and "retirement" facility for large animals abandoned as pets or show animals.

The two men often trained and provided animal actors for safe and humane movie work. In the film industry, the men were known as animal wranglers. They were in the Smokies to provide a mountain lion—Omar—and a bear—Gus—for a major adventure feature movie, *Dropped into Danger,* based on Jumper Herman's story. Friends of the Hardys, the two wranglers had invited the boys to work on the film with them.

"So you think a bear might have had something to do with Herman's disappearance?" Gene asked Joe.

"Well, the way I understand the story," Joe said,

"is that Jake Herman stole a huge collection of small archaeological treasures, right? Old coins, ancient gold jewelry, stuff like that."

"Right," Gene agreed. "He was thirty years old, and the robbery happened in Canada about twenty-five years ago."

"Then he flew his own small plane across the border," Frank added, remembering what he'd read in the movie script the night before, "smuggling all the loot into the United States."

"His plane supposedly crashed here in the Great Smoky Mountains," Joe said, "and he was never seen again. Maybe he finally met his match with a bear."

"But don't forget," Frank said. "Jumper was famous for pulling off daring crimes and never being caught for any of them. In fact, he got the nickname *Jumper* because he was a daring parachutist in the army. Maybe he ditched before the crash and has been living off the loot ever since."

"They found a few traces of his leather bag, but not the million dollars' worth of loot that was in it," Gene pointed out. "Who knows what happened. Maybe the movie will supply some answers."

"You guys have been here a couple of days," Lloyd said to Frank and Joe. "How do you like the work so far?"

"Outstanding," Joe answered. "Working with Gus and Omar is fun by itself. Working on a major movie will make it even better."

4

"Then let's go to work," Gene said. He handed each of the Hardys a worn suede bomber jacket and a wide-brimmed leather safari hat.

"Remember, you're in charge of the cooler containing food rewards," Lloyd added. "There's a list in the barn of who gets what and a shooting schedule for each animal. While we're at the shoot, you'll follow along in the script and help us with our cues."

"And anything we might need," Gene chimed in.

"The main thing to realize is that moviemaking isn't as glamorous as most people think," Lloyd pointed out. "It's mostly a waiting game. Hours of sitting around and waiting, and then a few minutes of work and intense concentration."

"None of us is on call every day," Gene said. "If you're not needed for wrangling, feel free to sign up as acting extras. That can be fun."

The four worked and trained the rest of the morning and afternoon. They were preparing for an evening shoot at a location set farther up the mountain. When they finished, Gene and Lloyd took Gus back to his traveling trailer, while Frank and Joe went to the barn next to it.

"This is a perfect setup," Frank said to his brother. Part of the film was being shot in the tiny mountain town of Crosscook and the surrounding countryside. So the movie studio had set up headquarters there.

The cast and crew stayed in town, in private homes, inns, and elaborate RVs. The animal wranglers and other stunt crew, security personnel, and administration staff stayed in small steel prefabricated houses that the studio had brought in and set up at the edge of town. All together the houses looked like an army barracks or a small campground.

"It is a perfect setup," Joe agreed. "The animals have their own familiar traveling trailers. And we've got this old barn to store the equipment and feed."

"And to use for rehearsing," Frank added as he watched Gene walk Gus up a ramp into the bear's trailer. Omar's trailer was parked nearby.

The Hardys packed the food that would be given to Gus while he worked. Then they walked about thirty yards from the barn and trailers to the house that the wranglers and the Hardys shared. At four-thirty they all changed into fresh jeans and shirts and began packing up for the short drive farther up the mountain.

"We've learned to take both trucks," Lloyd told them. "Gene and I will drive one and pull Gus's trailer. You two take the other."

Frank drove the second wrangler truck, following Gene out of the compound and up the mountainside.

They arrived at the location set in a large clearing in the mountain forest. At one end of the clearing was the plane crash set. On another section of the location was a copy of the isolated cabin where Jumper had supposedly hidden out for years. The shoot that evening would focus on scenes of Jumper's daughter searching for her father.

The wranglers parked their vehicles. While Gene checked on Gus, Lloyd showed the Hardys around. When they reached the edge of a ravine, they saw a man in a blue jumpsuit adjusting an elaborate rigging hanging from a crane.

"Terry!" Lloyd yelled. "I heard you were going to be on this shoot. Great working with you again."

The man left the crane setup and walked over. He appeared to be in his late twenties and had the compact, muscular body of a trained athlete. He had large dark eyes and was completely bald.

"Frank, Joe, this is Terry Lavring, one of the greatest stunt masters you'll ever work with," Lloyd said.

"Nice to meet you," Terry said. "Lloyd, you look scratched and bruised as usual. Where's Gene?"

"He's getting our bear settled," Lloyd said. "At least my wounds come from a reasonable source— a wild animal. Yours all happen because you insist on setting yourself on fire or jumping off buildings or whatever."

"Hey, once a chute cowboy, always a chute cowboy," Terry said, shrugging his shoulders.

"That's a stuntman who started out by jumping with parachutes," Lloyd explained to the Hardys.

"Now Terry's a master," Gene said, joining them. "Designs and creates incredible illusions."

"A true master," a familiar voice said. Everyone turned to see the beautiful face of Cleo Alexander. She gazed at them with large blue eyes, a surprising color because her hair, a short curly cap, was very dark brown.

Terry introduced everybody. "I'm sure you know this young lady from her Olympic gymnastic glory days and her two sports films. I've worked with her, and I'm telling you she's going to be a real movie star. And this is the film that will do it. She's playing Jumper's daughter, who goes to search for her dad when she's grown. Wait till you see what she's going to do. It'll knock you dead."

Cleo flashed a huge sparkling smile. "I hate to interrupt you all, but I really need to talk to you about the stunt, Terry." She seemed nervous.

"No problem," the stunt master said. "Okay, everybody—talk to you later."

The Hardys and the wranglers left Terry and Cleo and strolled around the set. "She's the one in the scene with Gus, right?" Joe asked.

"Yep," Gene answered. "The script has Gus chasing her. Let's get the fence coil unloaded. We need one of you to give us a hand."

"I'll do it," Joe offered.

"Have I got time to look around?" Frank asked.

"Sure," Lloyd said. "We've got about an hour before we need to set up."

Frank took a trail up the mountain to an observation area where others were seated on logs and benches. He looked back down on the clearing. The mountainside teemed with the activity of preparing for a movie shoot.

"It's amazing, isn't it?" a woman about forty years old said, plopping down next to him. "This is my fourth movie, and I never get tired of it."

"Are you an actress?" Frank asked, then introduced himself.

"Oh, my, no," she said. "I'm Sassy Leigh, a folklore professor at a college not far from here. I'm a consultant on the film because I'm considered sort of an expert on the legend of Jumper Herman."

Sassy was a pretty woman. She had a mane of hair streaked with several colors of dark red and gold. Her green eyes stared intently at Frank, as if she were trying to figure out *his* legend.

"I've read only a little about him," Frank said. "What's your expert conclusion about what happened?"

"Well, there are certainly lots of theories," Sassy said. "Some think Jumper survived and has been happily mocking the international authorities ever since.

"One of the most popular rumors has Jumper

meeting his fate with the Great Smoky Mountains version of Bigfoot," Sassy continued.

"There's a Smokies Bigfoot?" Frank asked.

"Oh, yes," she said. "They've had lots of sightings hereabouts."

"He's been written into the script, I'll bet," Frank said.

"Of course," Sassy said, smiling proudly. "I helped write that part." She smoothed the green sweater she wore over her jeans.

The sun dropped into the mist clinging to the blue-green ridge beyond, and the temperature seemed to drop a degree every minute.

"Well, I'd better get back to—" Frank's words stopped in his throat as a high scream tore through the cool mountain air from the set below.

Sassy's head whipped around. "What was that?" she asked. She sounded scared.

"Let's find out," Frank said. He and Sassy headed back down the trail with everyone else who had been sitting around them. After a few yards Frank left the crowd and raced through the meadow grass and mountain scrub that skirted the dense forest.

When he reached the forest that stood between him and the set, he decided to run around it. It was getting darker and he knew the dense forest could be a mazelike trap.

As he ran along the edge of the forest, a peculiar

smell drifted toward his nostrils. It was a sour, gamy, sweaty odor. Whew, Frank thought as the odor grew stronger. Smells like a cross between a zoo and the gym after a really rough basketball practice.

He could hear shouts ahead on the set. He stepped up his pace, running beside the huge trees. But he was distracted again by the odd smell and by a rustling from inside the forest. He decided that something must be running through the trees—running in the same direction he was, but four or five yards away on a parallel path.

He looked to his left, squinting to get a better view into the darkness of the forest. There were lots of shadowy shapes in there, and some of them seemed to move. And lots of crackling, whistling, whining sounds. Were they made by tree branches bending in the wind, Frank wondered. Or maybe the family of deer he had seen earlier bounding across the meadow?

It was the sudden rush toward him that caught him off guard—the huge form bursting from between two trees. Frank didn't have a chance. There was no warning, no time for defense. A beefy arm swung out of the large smelly mass in a huge arc.

2 Dropped into Danger

The sour, gamey smell thickened the air. Frank felt the heavy arm slam into his chest, leveling him with one powerful backhand blow.

Frank landed on his side and rolled a couple of times. Dazed, he watched his attacker run into the forest. He could barely make out the hulking shape.

He pulled himself to his knees and gasped for a breath of putrid air. After shaking his head a few times, he stood up and headed on toward the set at a slow trot.

"Frank!" Sassy called from behind. "Wait a minute. What happened?" she asked when she reached him. "Did you trip or something? I saw you get up."

"You didn't see me hit the ground?" Frank asked as they kept going. "You didn't see whoever—or whatever—it was that decked me?"

"What are you talking about?" Sassy asked. She sounded a little breathless, maybe from trying to keep up with Frank. "Someone knocked you down?"

They finally reached the edge of the location set. "Mmm-hmmm," Frank mumbled. Ahead, he spotted Joe and Lloyd. He really didn't want to get into a big conversation with Sassy right then. He wanted to find out who screamed—and why.

"There you are!" Joe said when Frank and Sassy joined them.

"What happened?" Frank asked. "We heard someone scream and got here as fast as we could." He decided to tell Joe about his attacker later.

"It was Cleo," Joe said, nodding toward the pretty young star. They watched as she paced back and forth. Cleo's personal assistant, Carmen, paced with her, and a small group of cast and crew members stood around, whispering to one another. Sassy wandered over toward the others.

"We don't know exactly what happened," Joe said in a low voice as he, Frank, and Lloyd sidled over toward Cleo. "That's the director, Dustin Bird, with her now."

Frank watched as the director started talking to Cleo. Dustin Bird was about sixty years old, dressed in jeans, a denim shirt, and a baseball cap. He had a rich British accent. "Come on, Cleo," Dustin said. "It's just a stupid joke. You know—everyone keeps talking about how this shoot is jinxed. Someone's just acting on the rumors, trying to rattle you, that's all."

"Well, it's working!" Cleo said, glaring at Dustin. She clenched and unclenched one hand over and over. As she resumed pacing again, a small wad of paper tumbled out of her hand.

As if he were picking up a grounder in left field, Joe scooped up the crinkled paper and stepped away with it. Turning his back, he smoothed the note and read it quickly.

Frank read over his brother's shoulder. The message was short and to the point. "Get out of this movie. Your life is in danger!"

Joe wadded up the note again and took it to Cleo. "You dropped this," he said.

Cleo gave Joe a shaky smile. "Thanks," she said. She started to stuff it into a leg pocket of her cargo slacks but stopped abruptly, glancing at the others.

"Did you all hear this?" she asked, her voice agitated. She read the note aloud. Several people gasped and some actually appeared afraid. Others chuckled.

"Cleo," Dustin said. "I'm telling you it's just a gag. Someone from publicity probably wrote it. It's good for business if we've got a threat in the news."

"Do you have any idea who wrote the note?" Frank asked Cleo. He and Joe moved closer. Carmen put an arm around Cleo's shoulders.

"No," Cleo said. "But whoever it was, he'll be sorry," she added.

"Where did you find the note?" Frank asked. "Was it delivered to your RV?" He knew that major stars had their own RVs when they went on location. The vehicles were personal retreats for the stars, somewhere they could go when they weren't needed for a particular scene.

"Yes," Cleo said, nodding at Frank. "I was over in makeup, and when I got back to my RV, this note was stuck under my door."

"Are you sure you don't know the handwriting?" Carmen asked.

Cleo's answer was cut off by Dustin. "Okay, that's it," he said. "Enough questions, enough excitement."

He took Cleo's hand and led her away. "Come on, dear," he said in a soothing voice. "Let's have some tea. I want you a little agitated for the next scene, but not hysterical." Carmen followed closely.

"Well," Frank said. "It looks like there's more going on here than we thought."

"Yeah," Lloyd added. "The movie plot isn't the only mystery around here."

"A weird thing happened to me, too," Frank said. "Let's get some supper at the truck and I'll tell you about it."

Food for the cast and crew was served several ways, depending on where they were filming. In the main compound, food was always available in the commissary, one of the temporary steel buildings the studio had brought in and set up.

When filming was on location up on the mountain, the studio set up a tent or parked a large catering truck nearby. Hot food, hot and cold drinks, and snacks were available at the truck all the time. Specific meals were very elaborate and delicious.

This time Frank, Joe, and Lloyd decided they just wanted tacos from the food truck. They parked themselves at one of the tables and dug in. A tall heater stood near them, keeping off the mountain chill.

"There you are," Gene said as he walked up a few minutes later to join them. "I figured I'd find you near the food," he added with a grin. "I heard what happened with Cleo. Did any of you see the note?"

"Joe and I did," Frank answered. "It was printed in block letters in pen, and the letters looked pretty shaky."

"Like maybe it was written with the left hand by a right-handed person," Joe added. "You know what I mean?"

"Yeah, I do," Gene said. "Gus broke my arm in a training session one time. I had to write with my left hand for a few weeks. It was pretty bad."

"Maybe the author was afraid Cleo might recognize the writing," Lloyd suggested.

"Or the note writer is simply smart enough to disguise himself—or herself," Frank suggested.

"So what do you think?" Gene asked. "Is it a real threat or a joke?"

"I don't know," Frank said. "I'd like to talk to Cleo again. I want to know whether this is the first threat she's had."

Joe turned to Frank. "Hey, you said you had another weird thing to tell us about."

Frank's attention went immediately to his encounter at the edge of the forest. Just remembering that gamy, wild smell seemed to fill his nostrils.

As Frank told the story, the animal wranglers exchanged glances. Finally Lloyd spoke up, "It was a bear, Frank. The size, the smell—it had to have been. It was probably startled by Cleo's scream."

"And you were lucky," Gene added. "It had to be either a young bear or a very old one. You might not be here to tell us about it otherwise."

"What's the matter, Frank?" Joe asked, studying his brother's puzzled expression.

"I thought it was a bear, too," Frank said, "until it ran off. It loped away—on two feet."

17

"Bears will do that once in a while," Lloyd said. "They get up on their hind legs as a sign of dominance and power. Maybe it stayed up a bit longer to make sure you got the message."

"Or maybe you didn't see it clearly," Gene offered. "It was pretty dark by then."

"You don't look convinced, Frank," Joe said. "Do you think it was a man?"

"I don't know," Frank said, shaking his head. "It was so big. It smelled like a wild animal, so you guys are probably right."

"Of course, there *is* another possibility," Joe said with a grin. "Big, hairy, smelly, runs on two legs, lives in the mountain forest . . ."

"I see where you're going," Frank said. "Bigfoot, right?"

As Joe shrugged his shoulders and grinned, a voice came over the loudspeaker, telling the crew to report to the location.

"Come on, guys, that's us," Gene said. "We'll get Gus and meet you on the set." They dumped their trash in the bin, and Gene and Lloyd left to get Gus from his trailer.

When Frank and Joe reported to the location, the film crew was gearing up to finish shooting the scene.

"So, it looks like Cleo's feeling better." Terry said, joining them. They all looked at the young star. A makeup artist was brushing powder on her face as the light director checked his settings.

"Did you hear about the note?" Joe asked.

"I sure did," Terry answered. "I kind of thought she might not want to finish this scene tonight. "She's got to be fully focused on the action, or it could be a disaster."

"How come she's doing her own stunt, anyway?" Joe asked.

"She's a gymnast, remember?" Terry reminded him. "Silver medal in the Olympics. She's stayed in shape and has it written into her contract that she does her own stunts if she wants."

"Here comes Gus," Frank reported.

The crowd assembled for the shoot formed a wide path for the wranglers and their charge. Gus was in a harness and leash, but he was calm and quiet. Whatever jumped me didn't look like Gus, Frank thought. He watched the large bear saunter by.

"Well, it's show time," Joe said, clapping his brother's shoulder. "Let's get to work."

"Me, too," Terry said. "Now that everyone's finished fussing around Cleo, I want to check *her* harness and leash. The script says that the bear chases her to the ravine and she jumps across it to escape. When she goes, I want to make sure she gets all the way across!"

The Hardys watched Terry as he clipped the wire to the harness Cleo wore under her jacket to support her across the ravine.

"Everybody ready?" the assistant director yelled. "Let's go!"

"Okay, let's film Gus first," Dustin said. "Then we'll do Cleo. Wranglers, are you ready? Let's do this in one shot. Make it good, Gus."

As if he understood, Gus rumbled agreeably and gave his head a mighty shake.

Frank and Joe cleared the location of all cast and crew. It didn't take much convincing for them to move way back. As an extra guarantee, Frank and Joe unrolled a coil of heavy metal fencing along both sides of the path Gus would run. Later the fence would be "erased" from the film so it wouldn't show in the final cut.

Then Joe and Lloyd walked Gus to the far end of the run, where Gus would begin. When they reached the spot Dustin had marked, they stopped. Lloyd removed Gus's harness and leash.

"Whenever you're ready," Dustin called to them.

"Okay, Gus," Gene yelled from beside Frank. "Let's go. Come on, boy. Come see me."

Even though Frank had seen Gus do this run a half-dozen times by now, he felt a wave of expectation billow in his chest.

Gus was in rare form—a wild bear determined to defend its territory. Or so it looked to the cast and crew. And so it would seem to the millions of moviegoers who would see Gus on screen.

Gus's run was perfect. It was better than it had been at any of the rehearsals. "I know this sounds crazy," Gene said, "but I swear he knows the difference between rehearsing and filming. When the lights go on, he seems to really understand what's happening."

Gus shook his huge woolly head and shot sprays of drool onto Frank's shirt. The odor was familiar. Maybe it was a bear that slammed me, Frank thought.

"That was outstanding," Dustin called out as the crew applauded. "It's definitely a keeper."

Frank and Joe wound the wire fencing back into a heavy coil and wrestled it onto a dolly. Pushing the dolly, Frank followed Gene, Lloyd, and Gus back to the wranglers' truck and trailer.

Next it was Cleo's turn. She would run the same path Gus had taken before coming to the small ravine for her daring leap. Later Dustin and the film editor would mix the two scenes together. When they were finished, it would look as if Gus were actually chasing Cleo.

Joe stayed to watch the filming of Cleo's part of the scene. The young star went to the end of the path Gus had taken during his shoot. Then she made a few practice runs to the edge of the ravine. At last she made the final run.

Joe admired the way she turned the run into a frightening scene. She looked back in terror, as if she actually saw Gus chasing her. Then her expression changed as she realized the ground ahead of her had opened up and she had to make a horrible decision. As she neared the ravine, she took a deep breath and launched herself over the chasm.

Joe could barely see the "invisible" cord that supported her. But above her, out of camera range, he could see the crane from which the cord was hung. As he watched the crane move slowly out over the ravine, he heard a gasp from behind him, then a growing murmur rumbling through the crowd of onlookers.

He looked back at Cleo, and his breath caught in his chest. She was no longer "flying" in a graceful leap over the ravine. Her body seemed to sag, then her legs twitched awkwardly. Her arms flailed in the air.

"No!" Joe called out. His chest felt tight as he raced to the edge of the ravine. It looked as if the cord holding her harness was giving way. Helpless, he watched as Cleo's body sagged once more and then plunged into the darkness.

3 The Eyes
at the Window

For the second time that evening, a scream rang out through the mountain mist. Cast and crew members raced to the edge of the ravine. It looked as if Cleo were attached to a long bungee cord, but one that wasn't bouncing back.

Joe could see that the young actress was still connected to the cord, and the cord was still threaded through the pulley. But the winch wasn't catching and holding the cord. The weight of her body was lengthening her lifeline as she plunged deeper into the ravine.

Joe rushed to Terry, who was battling with the mechanism that controlled the flying harness. "Push down this lever," Terry yelled. "The gear is stripped, and we have to pull her up manually."

Terry led Joe to the fail-safe backup system he had installed. Joe grabbed the lever and pushed down with all his strength. It seemed to be jammed. He took a deep breath and pushed again. Finally he felt it give. Terry turned the wheel that manipulated the cord. Joe took another deep breath—this time of relief—when he saw the cord connected to Cleo's harness begin moving up again.

As Joe and Terry strained to turn the wheel, a cheer burst through the mist and echoed around the ravine. Joe felt a rush of adrenaline as the taut cord pulled Cleo up into the light. Once her feet cleared the edge of the ravine, Terry secured the wheel. Then he swung the crane around so she dangled above them and the ground.

Joe and Terry reversed the wheel, lowering Cleo gently to safety.

"Good save." Joe heard Frank's voice behind him.

"Thanks," Joe said as he finally released the wheel. His shoulders ached, but he felt exhilarated. "Did you see that?" he asked.

"I sure did," Frank answered. "Gene and Lloyd took Gus back to the compound and released you and me until tomorrow, so I thought I'd watch the stunt. Got here just as you and Terry landed Cleo. What happened anyway?"

"I'm not sure," Joe said. "Let's go find out."

"You two go ahead," Terry said. "I'll be there in a minute. I have to get this rig secured."

Joe and Frank joined the small crowd that circled the young actress and Dustin. The production company's doctor, who was on-site for all location filming, also rushed to the actress.

Cleo hopped over to a bench and plopped down. Carmen hovered behind the bench and wrapped a sweater around Cleo's shoulders.

"It's my ankle," Cleo said in a soft voice. Her eyes crimped nearly shut as she tried to move her foot. "Yikes, I think it's broken."

The doctor gingerly touched Cleo's ankle and foot. "It's probably just a sprain, but I want an X ray to make sure," he told Dustin.

"There you are," Cleo said, when she spotted Joe. "One of my heroes. Something happened to the flying harness. It worked perfectly in rehearsal."

As she talked, the doctor slipped a temporary cast over her lower leg, snapping it snugly around her leg and ankle. "Ow," she complained. "That hurts."

"Okay, everyone," Dustin said to the small crowd. "That wraps it for tonight. Scene thirty-two at six-thirty tomorrow morning here. And I mean six-thirty—I need to get the morning mist." He and the doctor huddled for a private talk, and the crowd drifted away.

"Terry's looking over the rig now," Frank said,

sitting next to Cleo on the bench. He helped her get out of the harness and handed it to Joe.

"Did you feel anything strange before the cord gave way?" Joe asked. "Was it like a sudden jerk? Or was there a warning?"

"Everything felt great at first," Cleo said. "The jump was perfect, timed exactly right." Frank noticed that even though her words were matter-of-fact, she sounded very shaky and nervous.

"When did you realize something was wrong?" Joe asked, crouching in front of the bench.

"It was so sudden," Cleo said. Frank saw her shoulders ripple with a slight shiver. "I had no warning—not a clue."

"I wonder if it was an accident," Carmen muttered.

"That's enough," Cleo said, her eyes wide. She twisted around to stare at Carmen.

"What do you mean, Carmen?" Joe asked.

"I mean what I mean," Carmen said. "She's gotten threats, notes, phone calls. Now there's a so-called accident. What do *you* think it means?"

"Carmen," Cleo said, "I said that's enough—"

"Okay, honey," Dustin interrupted as he and the doctor rejoined them. "Doc's going to take you to the hospital in Crosscook. It's small, but he knows the guy who runs it and trusts him. They can do the X ray and if you need any major treatment, we'll fly you to a city tonight."

Before Frank or Joe could question Cleo further, she was carried away by the doctor. Carmen bustled along behind them.

"So what do you think?" Joe asked his brother as they walked back to Terry. "Do you suppose this is something more than an accident?"

"I'm not sure," Frank answered. "I thought I saw something when Cleo looked at Carmen. It was like she was trying to shut her up before she said any more."

"We need to talk to Cleo again," Joe decided.

Terry was still examining the flying harness rig when the Hardys joined him. Huge lights flooded the area with intense brightness. Joe handed over the harness Cleo had worn, and Terry checked it out. "I don't know, guys," he said. "It all looks okay so far. But something went wrong. I won't know what until I take everything apart and go over every inch of the assembly."

Frank helped the stunt master dismantle the rig while Joe gave the crane motor and transmission a thorough once-over. "Hey, look at this." Frank and Terry joined Joe at the front of the crane cab. A tiny rock was jammed into the gear assembly. One of the gears was bent into a flap over the stone.

"That's it!" Terry said. "Someone wedged that rock in there, and—"

"Not so fast," Joe interrupted. "That really could

be an accident. This rig was brought up the mountain in a semi, right?"

"Yeah," Terry said, nodding. "That one." He pointed to a tractor trailer parked in the vehicle area not far from where they stood.

"Well, this isn't exactly a nice asphalt highway up here," Joe pointed out. "You could have picked up that rock just driving it out of the semi and over here."

"You're right," Terry agreed. "It was probably some sort of mechanical failure." His shoulders slumped in a dejected posture. "All those dry runs—so perfect, not a hitch."

"This might be something," Frank said. He held the two pieces of the harness connection that he'd just taken apart. It was a small gear assembly that looked as if a couple of the gear teeth were missing.

"This is a brand-new rig," Terry said, examining the piece that Frank handed him. "I assembled it myself. I checked it before every rehearsal and just before the stunt."

"And you never left the rig alone after your final check?" Frank asked.

"Two or three minutes, maybe," Terry said. "A quick phone call—something about doing a publicity appearance tomorrow. I blew them off because I didn't want to leave the rig."

"It would take longer than that to tamper with this," Joe concluded.

"Unless someone knew exactly what to do," Frank said. "And where."

"You mean someone who knows the flying stunt?" Terry said. "That's not possible. This is my rig. I created it. I guess if someone knew stunts, they might be able to figure it out." He looked anywhere but at Frank. It was as if he didn't want to meet Frank's gaze. Was he hiding something or just embarrassed because the stunt had failed?

"Look, I've got to talk to Cleo," Terry said. "Where is she?"

Frank told Terry that Cleo had been taken to the hospital.

"Okay," Terry said. His body pounced into action. "I'm going to the hospital. I have to talk to her."

"Sounds like a plan," Joe said. "We'll go with you."

"I was hoping you'd say that," Terry said. "Gene and Lloyd say you guys are detectives." Both boys nodded. "Looks like I've got a case for you. Help me find out what happened, will you?"

"We'll give it a shot," Frank said.

They finished dismantling the rig and packed it into the semi. Then Terry drove the crane into the truck and locked the rear and front doors.

The three got into one of the animal wrangler trucks. Frank started it up and took off down the winding drive.

Terry was the navigator, following a map. It was very dark. A few stars glinted in the occasional patches of sky they saw. But most of the time they were surrounded by the mountain forest. The high beams made a funnel of eerie light on the deserted dirt road.

"The hospital is about twenty miles from here," Terry said, studying the map. "Wait a minute. I know where we are. Stop!"

Frank hit the brakes, and pine needles and dirt swirled in the light ahead of them.

"I have to show you guys something," Terry said. "Turn right here."

Frank pulled off the mountain road onto an even more primitive path that led deep into the forest. He skillfully guided the truck through ruts and over fallen branches as they wound up the side of another mountain ridge.

"There," Terry said. "That's it." He pointed out the window into the blackness.

"Uh, *what's* it?" Joe said, straining his eyes.

"Where's your flashlight?" Terry said.

Frank opened the metal box on the seat beside him and passed heavy-duty lanterns to Terry and Joe.

"There," Terry said. "See that path?" He waved his light toward a narrow strip of land where the ground cover was slightly stomped down.

"I suppose you could call it that," Joe said,

his light joining Terry's. "Where does it go?"

"Follow me," the stunt master said, jumping down from the truck and starting up the trail. They hadn't gone far into the woods when Terry swung his light upward. A dark silhouette filled the beam. "I knew I'd find it," he said, continuing along the path.

Frank and Joe followed until they reached a dirty, dilapidated mountain shack. It was obviously abandoned. What was once the floor of a small porch had sagged so deeply in the middle that the boards were cracked. When the floor boards had broken, the columns holding the porch roof had caved in, bringing the middle of the roof down to a sharp V.

The shack had had a chimney because large charred stones were lying on the roof. Amazingly, the front door was intact and tightly shut. Terry vaulted over the broken porch and pushed open the door. The Hardys followed.

"Whoa," Joe said. "What's that smell?"

"It's gross," Terry said. "Smells like something died."

The familiar odor filled Frank's nostrils. "This is what I smelled when that bear or whatever knocked into me. Watch yourselves. There might be one lurking nearby."

Although he was sure no one lived here any longer, Frank still felt as if he should whisper. He was wary, his eyes scanning the room. There was something about the shack that gave him the feeling that they were being watched.

"What is this place?" he asked in a hushed voice.

"Rumor is that it was Jumper Herman's hideout," Terry said, his voice low. Something fluttered in the fireplace on the far wall, and Frank's breath caught in his throat. Then whatever it was scampered up the chimney and out on to the roof.

"All right!" Joe said, his voice a little louder than the others. "So let's look around. It's probably been searched over and over the last couple of decades, but you never know . . ."

"Yeah—it hasn't been explored by the Hardys, right?" Terry said.

"True," Frank agreed. "Although if we do find something, we won't know if it was left by Jumper or by someone else."

Frank flashed his light slowly around the room. A few wood chairs stood in heaps of leaves and sticks and dirt. What might have passed for a bed—a long wooden platform—was in a corner. A table lay on its side near the fireplace.

As he swung his light past the grimy window in the far wall, something caught Frank's eye. Although he had moved the light past the window, his eyes stayed trained on the cloudy glass panes.

Slowly, he brought the light back and then stood very still. He tried not to move a cell of his body. The window panes were veiled with dirt, but they couldn't mask what Frank had seen. Two yellow eyes glinted through the glass, their unblinking stare fixed directly on him.

4 Banned from the Set

Frank's eyes locked with the yellow eyes staring into the abandoned shack. Suddenly the staring game was over—Frank had won. The yellow eyes blinked and disappeared.

Frank raced to the window and held his light high against the dirty glass.

"What did you see?" Joe asked, rushing to join his brother.

Frank told the others what had happened.

"Was it a bear, do you think?" Terry asked.

"Maybe—or something less menacing. A deer, even," Frank suggested.

"Let's check it out," Joe said. "It blinked first, so it's probably not in attack mode."

"And there are three of us, right?" Terry said.

"Okay," Frank agreed. "But remember, whatever it is, it's not Gus or Omar. We're talking wild animal here." The three grabbed makeshift weapons of broken chair legs and other pieces of wood lying on the floor.

Frank led the others slowly around the shack to the back. The air was thick with that sweaty smell. The ground was trampled beneath the window, and there seemed to be an escape route cleared into the woods. But they saw nothing as they shone their lights into the quiet blackness.

"Shhh," Frank said, motioning to the others to stop.

They stood very still for a few moments. Frank heard something moving away from them in the woods. Joe and Terry nodded, indicating they had heard it, too. The sound grew fainter and finally faded away.

Frank strained to hear more. For a few minutes it was so quiet that he heard only the other two breathing. Then the silence was broken by a raccoon skittering across the shack roof and dropping to the ground.

"Maybe that's what you saw," Terry said. "Looks like this one's heading out after his buddy."

"Could be," Frank mumbled. He started along the trampled path leading away from the shack window. The odor was strong.

35

Those don't look like raccoon prints, he told himself as his light played along a strange indentation. "Over here," he called to the others. "Look at this." Frank pointed out two large dents in the soil. They looked like huge pawprints. Nearby a tuft of fur clung to a brambly thistle.

"Whoa," Terry said. "It *was* a bear. Look at the size of those prints!"

Joe took a tape measure from his pocket and checked the dimensions of the prints, writing the numbers in a small notebook. "Would you believe twenty inches long by eight inches wide?" he asked the others. He also drew a rough sketch of the shape of the prints. "That's some big bear," he added, jamming the notebook and pen back into his jeans pocket.

"And a weird-colored one, too," Frank said, picking the piece of brown fur off the thistle.

"Gene and Lloyd can probably help us identify it," Joe pointed out.

The three spent a few minutes more looking around the inside of the shack but found nothing. Then they returned to the truck, and Frank drove them back down the overgrown path to the dirt road leading to Crosscook.

"We shouldn't have any trouble finding the hospital," Frank said as they pulled into a small residential area. "In a town this small, there's usually a sign with directions posted on the edge of town."

"You're right," Terry said. "There it is." Frank slowed the truck so they could read the information. Three green-and-yellow signs were stacked on a pole. One said Welcome to Crosscook. One said Sheriff, with an arrow pointing right. And one said Hospital, with an arrow pointing left.

Frank turned left and four blocks later, pulled into the hospital parking lot. The hospital lobby was small but new and sparkling clean. After a quick check at the Information desk, the Hardys and Terry headed for the elevator.

Cleo was on the fourth floor—the top floor—in a private room in the corner. Windows on two walls looked out onto the quiet dark streets of Crosscook. The room was not very big, but it was furnished more like a living room with a bed than like a regular hospital room.

"Oh, I'm so glad you came!" Cleo said when they walked in. She was still wearing her pink sweatsuit. "Can you believe this place? Not bad for a town halfway up a mountain."

Cleo sat in a dark blue velvet recliner in the corner of the room. Her bandaged ankle appeared to be very swollen, and a pair of crutches leaned against the wall next to the chair. There were already three bouquets of flowers on tables around the room.

"So how are you feeling, kiddo?" Terry asked.

"Right now I feel wonderful," Cleo said, "but

they gave me some pretty strong medicine. I was thrilled to hear that my ankle isn't broken. It's just a bad sprain. I've had my share of those—one more won't kill me. They're making me stay overnight for observation—to make sure everything else is okay. I'll be out for a few days, but not out of the movie."

"That's good," Terry said. "I feel really bad about what happened."

"Hey, it wasn't your fault," Cleo said. Her face then twisted into a mean expression. "It wasn't, right?" she repeated.

"No, no," Terry assured her. "Well, actually we're not sure exactly what did happen."

Cleo's face brightened again. "I was just kidding—see what a good actress I am?" She flashed them all the famous wide grin that they had seen on magazine covers. "So what do you think happened?"

Terry glanced at Frank and Joe as if to ask how much he should say. Frank pulled up a chair and sat next to Cleo.

"You might be able to help us piece that together," Frank said. "The note you received earlier—you said you didn't know who might have sent it to you."

"That's right," Cleo said. Her warm smile froze and her eyes widened. "You're not saying . . ." She gazed at the others. "Wait a minute." She squirmed in her chair.

"Don't get excited, honey," Terry said.

"Are you saying that what happened to me during the stunt *wasn't* an accident?" Cleo asked Frank.

"Let's just say we're trying to look at all sides of this," Frank said.

Joe crouched next to Cleo's chair. "We just want to make sure there's no connection between the threats you've been getting and the stunt failure," he said.

"Who are you guys anyway?" Cleo said. "What's your interest in all this?"

Quickly Terry filled her in on the Hardys' background. He added that he had asked them to help him investigate what happened to the stunt. "Tell them anything you can think of that might help," he urged her. "And I'm not just talking about what happened with the flying rig. If you're in danger, that's more important to me than any stunt."

"I've trusted you with my life several times," Cleo said. "If you say the Hardys are okay, they must be. So how can I help?"

"Your assistant, Carmen, said you'd received other notes, letters, threatening phone calls," Frank said. "Tell us about those."

"I don't know what to tell you really," Cleo said. "I got a couple of letters right after the studio announced that I was in the movie. Then while we did some work on the sets in the studio, I got four phone calls. They were just quick messages, and the caller hung up right away."

"Did you report any of this to the police or studio security?" Frank asked.

"You may not know this," Cleo said, "but sports stars get threats all the time. I got stuff like this when I was in gymnastics—and especially when I was on the Olympic team. The mail was about equally divided between love letters and hate mail. When the first letter came, I didn't really pay much attention to it."

"So you never reported any of it?" Terry asked.

"The letter and notes didn't bother me so much, but when the phone calls started, I got a little scared. Hearing an actual voice on the phone . . . It made it more real, you know? So I told my agent and the head of studio security. They said they'd take care of it, and I figured they did. All the threats stopped for a couple of months . . . until today."

"And you didn't recognize the voice?" Frank asked.

"No," Cleo answered. "It was disguised. I couldn't tell if it was a man or woman, young or old . . . nothing."

Cleo looked out the window and repeated, "But the phone calls did scare me."

"And no one ever traced any of the threats?" Joe asked. "You have no idea who's doing this?"

"No," Cleo said. Her eyes started to fill with tears, but she shook her head. "Just some nut case, I guess. I thought it was over until I found that note under my door. It was such a shock, I panicked. Who could it be?" she said almost to herself.

Cleo became more agitated as she talked, and Terry seemed to want to lighten her mood. "Hey, maybe it's Jumper himself," he said with a grin. "A lot of people think the production is jinxed by old Jumper's ghost, still haunting these mountains."

"Don't even kid about that!" Cleo said with a shudder. "We can fight a person at least. It's hard to fight a ghost."

"Cleo, if there's anything you can tell us that might help," Frank began.

"Hey, ease up on her," Terry interrupted. "Can't you see she's upset. Let's talk about something else."

"I thought you wanted to talk to her about the stunt," Joe pointed out.

"Well, we talked to her," Terry said. "She doesn't know anything. End of subject."

"Hey, Terry, what's up?" Frank asked quietly. "Don't you want to know whether someone's trying to shut down the production? And if so, who?"

"And why?" Joe added.

Terry stared out the window and didn't say anything. Finally he turned back. "Look, this isn't the first time one of my stunts has failed on this production," he said.

"Terry," Cleo said. "It's okay. No one blames you."

"Yes, they do," Terry said. "The plane crash and parachuting stunt was a mess. And it cost the studio a lot of money in down time. There are a lot of people who probably think *I'm* the jinx—"

"I disagree," Cleo interrupted. "You're definitely not responsible for the notes and phone calls I've been getting. And you didn't tell people to say they had seen Bigfoot in the woods."

Cleo stood up and hopped over to the bed. "And, Terry, I know you make jokes about it, but some people have actually said they've seen the ghost of Jumper Herman. All movie sets have superstitions and rumors and jinxes. But this is the worst I've ever seen. You know, I wouldn't be too unhappy if they just closed down the production."

"What are you all doing here?" Cleo's personal assistant, Carmen, said as she bustled into the room. "She's supposed to be resting."

As Cleo lay back on her pillows, Carmen turned to Terry. "Get out of here," she said. "Haven't you done enough today. You nearly killed her with your stupid flying stunt. Come on. All of you—out!"

"Cleo, if you think of anything, let us know," Joe

called back as the Hardys and Terry left the hospital room.

In the parking lot Frank looked up at Cleo's window. "You know, she did act really scared when she was talking about some of the stuff happening on this mountain," he said.

"Yeah." Joe nodded. "But I saw the same expression on her face earlier tonight during the shoot. It was when she was supposedly running from Gus— and that time she was just acting."

The ride back to the studio compound was quiet. Frank realized how tired he was. Wrangling bears and pumas on a movie set could be pretty hard work. As Frank pulled through the gates of the compound, two studio security guards stepped in front of the truck and held up their hands.

"What's happening here?" Joe wondered out loud from the backseat.

Frank eased the truck to a stop and rolled down his window. But the guards went to the passenger side and opened the door.

"Terry Lavring?" one of the guards said.

"Yes," Terry answered.

"Step out of the truck, please," the guard said.

Terry and the Hardys got out of the truck. Frank walked around to where Terry and Joe stood. "What's the problem, Officer?" Frank asked.

"Our business is with Mr. Lavring," the guard

said. Then he turned to Terry. Frank watched in astonishment as the guard spoke: "Mr. Lavring, we have been ordered to inform you that your services on this film have been terminated, effective immediately."

5 Is Bigfoot Afoot?

"What are you talking about!" Terry said. "Fired! No way. Is this some kind of joke?"

"It is no joke, sir," the security guard said. "You are officially off the production as of this moment. Please leave the premises now."

"This is ridiculous," Terry said. He started to walk down the road, but the guard stepped in front of him and blocked his path. "Get out of my way. I'm going to my house. I'll straighten this all out with Dustin in the morning."

"Your house has been cleared, Mr. Lavring," the guard informed him. "All your personal belongings have been packed in boxes. We will escort you to your house and assist you in packing the boxes into the tractor trailer you drove here. Then you must leave. You will no longer be allowed on studio property."

"What about my equipment, my rigs?" Terry asked.

"The producer's staff is going through everything right now. Studio property will be retained. Everything else will be shipped to your ranch."

"Come on," Terry said. "At least let me supervise the packing. They could damage my equipment. If anything happens to my property, the studio is in for the lawsuit of the century!"

"We'll help you pack up," Joe said.

"I'm sorry, sir," the guard said to Joe. "We will escort Mr. Lavring. It would be best if you just went to your quarters."

"Go on, guys," Terry said. "We're not going to get anywhere with these two. Don't worry about me—I'll contact you tomorrow."

Terry stomped off down the road, the two guards hurrying to keep up. The Hardys got back in the truck and drove to their house. As Frank parked the truck, Gene and Lloyd came out to greet them.

"Terry just got fired," Frank told them.

"We know," Lloyd said. "We're glad you're back. Berk Shearer is inside."

"The actor who's playing Jumper?" Joe asked. "He came back out here from town?"

"That's right," Lloyd answered. "He couldn't sleep, so he came to talk. Go figure."

When they went inside, Berk was sitting at the kitchen table. Joe figured he was probably in his late twenties. He didn't look like a movie star, but he did bear a slight resemblance to the pictures the Hardys had seen of Jumper Herman.

Gene introduced the Hardys to Berk, cutting slabs of cherry pie for the five of them.

"So you heard about Terry getting fired," Frank said.

"We sure did—you missed all the fireworks," Gene reported. "After you three left, Dustin went nuts, ranting about how if there *was* a jinx on this production, it was Terry and his stunts. He was even talking like he thought Terry might be intentionally sabotaging the production."

"The producers talked to the studio head a couple of times—he's back in L.A.," Lloyd added. "The next thing we knew, Terry was out. The set designer told us, and he got the story from Dustin's assistant."

"You know, I like Terry," Gene said, "and he's got a great reputation in the business. But we don't really know him all that well."

"Yeah, but I can't believe he's responsible for any of the problems they've been having," Lloyd said. "We've worked with him before, and he's always been great. No problems at all."

"Why would he sabotage a movie he's working on?" Frank wondered out loud. "Does he have any history with Dustin or anyone else connected with the movie?"

"I don't think so," Gene said. "He told us this is the first time he's worked for this studio."

"I've never worked with him before," Berk said. "But I've heard he's really good."

"It looks as if you won't get a chance to work with him on this film, either," Frank said. "Who'll take over the stunts? Is this going to throw a kink in the shooting schedule?"

"Dustin's flying in someone he knows and has worked with a lot," Lloyd said. "Most of the big stunts are already shot, anyway."

"Well, tomorrow should be great," Joe said. He took a small notebook from his pocket and skimmed his notes. "It's the scene right after Jumper ditches the plane. He's hurt his leg, and he's knocked out. Then he comes to, checks out his leg, and gets out of the parachute. All this time, Omar is looking down on him from a nearby bluff."

"And Jumper—I—don't know I'm being watched," Berk said in a low, spooky voice. He stood up. "I take a few hesitant steps." He began limping around the kitchen. "Where's my bag, where's that loot?"

"It's dark, right?" Frank asked.

"Right," Berk said. "Nothing but moonlight, but there's plenty of that. I have no flashlight or anything. And I'm beating the bushes, looking for my leather bag."

"Which may have spilled out some of the treasures," Gene observed.

"True," Joe agreed. "So he's frantically searching, and suddenly he hears a low growl."

"Omar's big moment," Lloyd said with a grin.

"You bet," Joe said, closing the notebook.

"Well, I'm going to head back into town," Berk said. "It's really late now."

"He's staying at the inn," Gene pointed out. He walked Berk to the door, saying, "See you tomorrow. It'll be a great scene."

"Let's hope," Berk said with a smile.

After he left, the Hardys and the wranglers sat up a couple of minutes longer and talked about Terry and his firing.

"Cleo's definitely not going to like it," Lloyd said. "She and Terry are pretty close."

"Speaking of Cleo," Frank said. He told the wranglers about the hospital visit.

"I'm glad she's going to be back on the set soon," Gene said. "She's got guts to be willing to keep at it in spite of the threats."

"That reminds me," Frank said, reaching into his pocket. "What kind of animal has hair like this?" he asked, showing Gene and Lloyd the dark tuft of fur he had found near the abandoned shack.

"A bear, I suppose," Lloyd said, "but I'm not sure of the color. It's not really black. Maybe a cub before its mature hair grows in."

"I don't think it was a cub," Joe said. "Not with these footprints." He showed the wranglers the drawing and dimensions he'd recorded.

The Hardys told Gene and Lloyd about the abandoned shack. "The strangest thing was the smell," Frank concluded. "I swear it was the same odor that bear had when it slammed into me earlier."

Gene got an envelope and slipped the tufts of fur into it. "I'll check this out under the microscope I keep for emergency medical situations," he said. "See if I can identify it."

"Well, guys, we need to get some sleep," Lloyd said as he stood up from the table. "Joe, tomorrow morning you work with us—we shoot the scene with Omar at six-thirty. I need you rested and alert."

"I'll be ready," Joe said. His eyes shone with excitement. "I can't wait!"

"I'm going to use the time off tomorrow to follow some leads," Frank said. "I want to talk to some of the cast and crew."

Gene and Lloyd went out to the trailers to check Gus and Omar before they retired to their rooms. Frank and Joe grabbed some bottles of water and went to the bedroom they shared.

"Man, this bed feels good," Frank said as he sank into the mattress.

"Agreed," Joe called out from his bed.

The last thing Frank saw before his eyes shut was the glowing clock face, its hands pointing at twelve.

The first thing Frank saw when his eyes opened was the clock showing him it was one-twenty. What was that? A noise outside? he thought. Or was it just a dream? He thought about the yellow eyes at the shack window and could almost feel the impact of the large animal that knocked him down.

"I wonder . . ." he mumbled as he got out of bed.

He went to the window and looked out. A beam of light from the security lamp on the barn lit a path behind the little steel house. He saw nothing unusual out there.

Frank sat at a small desk in front of the window and opened his laptop. In minutes he had accessed the Internet and was searching for information about Bigfoot.

"Whoa," he whispered to himself. There were nearly a hundred and fifty thousand web sites about a Bigfoot monster, with reports from dozens of states and nearly every continent.

He narrowed his search to Bigfoot/Tennessee. Lists of research summaries, fuzzy photos, and reports of sightings appeared. Attacks and damage supposedly caused by Bigfoot creatures from seven to nine feet tall were described. There were also photos of what were supposed to be monster footprints and tufts of fur. Several sighters mentioned a foul odor—the Bigfoot in the Florida Everglades was even nicknamed Skunk Ape.

Frank combed his hand through his hair. Nah, he thought as he leaned back in the chair. It couldn't be . . .

A shuffling noise outdoors stopped his thoughts instantly. He sat up straight, focused on the night sounds. Cautiously, he stepped to the window and pulled the curtain aside. His eyes adjusted to the darkness, but he still saw nothing unusual outside.

As he turned away, he heard another noise, like the creaky snap of breaking wood. He pulled on his jacket and started for the door.

"Hey, what's up?" Joe asked sleepily as he raised up on his elbows.

"I heard something outside," Frank said.

"I'm right with you," Joe said. After bolting from bed, he pulled on jeans and a sweatshirt and followed Frank.

The night air was crisp, and the thin mist made everything seem blue-grayish and blurry. Frank pointed to himself and motioned toward the barn. Joe nodded and gestured that he would check around the house.

They split up, and Frank crept beside the bushes along the path to the barn. He noticed there were no strange vehicles in sight, but he still had the feeling someone—or something—was trespassing.

As he reached the corner of the barn, all his senses were on high alert. He was barely breathing, and his heart pounded in his chest. Choosing each step carefully, Frank started around the corner.

With a rush through the gray-blue veil of mist, a large blurry form loped away from the barn toward the animal trailers. The nervous cry of a mountain lion broke the stillness.

Frank started after the intruder. But as he left the protective covering of the barn, he felt a blow to the back of his head and saw bright lights shoot through his brain. He dropped to his knees, and as he fell, the sickening feeling of losing consciousness rippled through his body.

6 Or Is It a Ghost?

As Frank headed toward the barn, Joe circled the house. The nighttime mountain mist made all the outlines and landmarks fuzzy. He moved slowly, not wanting to give himself away by using a flashlight.

The penetrating whine of a mountain lion pierced the air and shot down Joe's spine. He rushed toward the animal trailers but stumbled over a heap on the ground.

"Frank! Frank!" Joe called as he realized whom he had tripped over. He felt his brother's pulse and was relieved to feel a normal beat.

"Man, what hit me?" Frank wondered, coming to.

"I don't know," Joe said. "I was behind the

house when I thought I heard Omar crying. I was heading toward the trailers when I found you knocked out."

"Yeah, I heard that cry, too," Frank said, shaking his head. "And I saw something run from the barn. It was headed straight for the trailers."

"I'm on it," Joe said. "You stay here and catch your breath."

"Are you kidding?" Frank said. "You're not going without me. Come on."

When they reached the animal trailers, all was well. Awakened by Omar's cry, Gene was tending to Gus, and Lloyd was checking Omar. Frank told the wranglers what had happened.

Relieved that their animal stars were unharmed, Gene and Lloyd decided to bunk with Omar and Gus for the rest of the night. Frank and Joe returned to the house and called the studio security chief to report Frank's assault.

Two security officers came over immediately to interview the Hardys, Gene, and Lloyd. Then the officers and Joe searched the area while the doctor examined Frank.

"So what did the doctor say?" Joe asked, when he finally returned to bed.

"I'll live," Frank said, touching the lump on his head. "Did you find anything out there?"

"Not really," Joe said. "It looks like someone tried to break into the barn. There's a piece of siding ripped off. Gene and the security guys think it might have been done by a wild animal."

"I'm going to crash," Frank said, falling back on his bed.

"It's three o'clock," Joe added. "Gene and Lloyd got our start time moved to eight, but that's still going to roll around pretty quick."

"Since I'm not needed tomorrow, I'm going to sign up as an extra," Frank said. "I want to hang around the set to talk to the cast and crew about what's been going on."

Tuesday morning the four wranglers grabbed a quick breakfast. They resolved to get more food from the commissary when they got to the location.

Gene and Lloyd packed up Omar and drove the trailer to the location up the mountain. Joe followed in one of the wrangler trucks.

Frank felt better. He unloaded the shipment of feed that arrived at eight-thirty. Then he drove the other truck up to the location.

When Frank reached the mountainside set, he went to the assistant director's trailer and signed in for duty as an extra. He was assigned the part of a reporter for a press conference scene later that day. He'd have no lines, just be part of the press crowd.

Frank's next stop was to wardrobe to get his costume for the part. The wardrobe mistress picked out a suit for Frank to wear during the filming. A small plastic press badge was clipped to the jacket pocket.

He wandered over to join a gathering near the commissary. He recognized the lighting director, a cameraman, a few other extras, Sassy Leigh, and Berk Shearer. Sassy sat on a wooden bench and moved over to make room for Frank. They were all talking about Cleo's note from the day before.

"So who do you think's behind all this?" Frank asked the group.

"Who—or what," Sassy said with a sly smile.

"There she goes again," the lighting director said with a chuckle.

"It's the ghost of Jumper Herman," one of the extras said, imitating Sassy.

"No—it's Bigfoot," the cameraman chimed in.

Several people applauded, and others laughed. Even Sassy laughed. "Okay, okay, give me a break. They all think I'm nuts," she said to Frank.

"So your guess is that Bigfoot or Jumper's ghost has been causing all the trouble around here," Frank concluded.

"Now, I wouldn't go that far," Sassy said. "Let's put it this way. A good folklorist gathers the legends and studies the documentation. A great folklorist keeps an open mind."

"What got you into folklore anyway?" Berk asked.

Sassy put down her neon purple clipboard and leaned back with a dreamy look. Tiny lines angled out from the corner of her eyes as she smiled.

"You know, I used to be really skeptical about so-called monsters—the Loch Ness serpent and, yes, Bigfoot. I always figured they were hoaxes. But the more I examined the evidence and the more people I interviewed—well, let's just say I think the creatures' existence is definitely possible."

"Talking about Bigfoot again, Sassy?" Cleo's voice immediately drew the group's attention, as she pulled up in an electric golf cart.

Frank stood and offered his seat on the bench to Cleo. She limped over, her foot encased in a temporary cast fastened with Velcro. The cast was the same bright red as her windsuit. She gave him a nervous smile.

The group talked about Cleo's accident, several people telling where they were and what they saw. Frank asked questions, but learned nothing. No one saw anyone tampering with the stunt rigging or Cleo's harness. As the others talked, he noticed that the conversation made Cleo nervous.

"You were asking earlier who you thought is behind all the problems with this shoot," one of the extras said to Frank. "If you ask me, someone ought to take a close look at Terry Lavring."

"Oh, come on," Cleo said. Her cheeks flushed,

and her eyes flashed with quick anger. "I've worked with Terry before. He would never set out to ruin a film. I don't believe it for a minute."

"What makes you think he has something to do with it?" Frank asked the young man.

"Hey, he's a master of illusions and stunts, right?" the props assistant answered. "Who better to make us think we're seeing ghosts and monsters?"

"But you don't have any real proof that he has done anything suspicious, right?" Frank asked.

"Of course he doesn't," Cleo said. "Come on, let's change the subject." She shook her head and pine needles that had fallen from the tree above flew off her hair.

"I heard they decided to rewrite the script so you won't be sidelined," Berk said to Cleo.

"That's right," Cleo said, brushing her hair with her hand. "While I'm looking for dear old dad, I'm going to fall and sprain my ankle. That way, as long as I feel up to it, we can still keep shooting."

"Well, looks like you all won't be shooting before lunch," Sassy said, checking her watch. "It's past noon now."

"That's movie business," the cameraman said, standing. "Hurry up and wait, hurry up and wait."

"I'm going to check in," one of the extras said. "See if they've got a new schedule yet." Several of the others left with him.

"How about some lunch, Cleo?" Berk asked, standing.

"No thanks," she said. "I think I'll go to my home away from home and rest my leg." With her back to Berk and Sassy, she looked intently at Frank. He could tell she was signaling with her eyes for him to follow her.

"You need any help?" Sassy asked.

"No, I'll be okay," Cleo answered. "Carmen is waiting for me there. Thanks." With a last long look at Frank, she climbed into the golf cart. Then she drove off toward a cluster of expensive, luxury recreational vehicles. The celebrity RVs were parked just inside the edge of the woods.

"Okay, Berk," Sassy said. "I have to meet with wardrobe about the changes to the Bigfoot costume. But I've got time for a quick cup of tea first. Let's go."

As soon as everyone else in the group had gone, Frank went to Cleo's RV. Even though it was nearly noon, tall trees cast huge shadows across the area.

"I'm so glad you came," Cleo said when she saw Frank. "Do you have a few minutes? You said you wanted to see the other notes I received."

"That'd be great," Frank said.

It was dark inside the RV. Cleo turned on the lights, saying, "I sent Carmen to the beauty salon this morning. She's been driving me crazy with her worrying. In fact, she hasn't even seen all these messages."

Cleo unlocked a drawer in the small desk in the main room of the vehicle and took out a small stack of paper. "Some of these are notes, some are phone messages that I wrote down after I heard them," she said, handing the stack to Frank. "How about a soda?"

"Thanks," Frank said, sitting in a large armchair. He began reading the notes: "Do not make 'Dropped into Danger' or you'll find out what that title means!" "You'll never get out of Tennessee alive."

"I got some of those phone messages before I left California," Cleo said, handing Frank his soda. "I think I know who's doing it, too. No one else took the threats seriously. Then when Terry brought you and your brother to the hospital, I knew I could confide in you. You will help, won't you?"

Frank looked at the young star. Her hands trembled, and for a moment he thought she was going to cry. "I'll do what I can," he said. "Who do you think is threatening you?"

Cleo leaned toward him and spoke very low. "It's Jumper," she said. "It's Jumper Herman's ghost."

Frank tried not to let the disappointment show on his face. He knew that whatever had knocked him down the night before, it was no ghost.

"You do believe me, don't you?" Cleo asked, her voice still low. "I've seen him a lot. He hangs around the set, but he stays in the shadows. Once I saw him at the back of the wardrobe trailer, and two days ago, I saw him walking across the road. I know he's a ghost, but for some reason he doesn't want the film made. You can find out why, right?"

"Anything's possible, Cleo, but . . ." Frank paused and turned toward the window. He wasn't sure, but he thought he'd heard something outside. He didn't want to mention it, because he didn't want to scare Cleo.

For a moment it was very still, then dark. The lights had suddenly gone out. The deep forest shadows blocked all sun from the room.

Cleo's frightened gasp broke the silence. "The lights," she whispered. "What happened?"

"Stay here," Frank whispered back. "Don't say anything."

Quietly, Frank got out of the chair. Carefully pacing each step, he walked to the door and listened. He heard nothing outside except the distant muffled sound of people talking.

Then a fluttering noise from behind him captured his attention. He turned around. He could barely see Cleo in the darkness. She was pushing herself back into her chair as if she were trying to disappear into the upholstery.

"No," she said. It was almost like a low moan. "No," she repeated. "Go away."

There was something about her voice that made the hair on Frank's arms bristle. Although her voice was low, the fear in it made a terrifying sound—far worse than a scream.

Frank followed her gaze down the long hallway. A dim greenish light filtered through the air as the pale image of Jumper Herman inched slowly toward them.

7 Stop, Thief!

With a jolt, Frank realized he was holding his breath. The shock of seeing Jumper's ghost floating toward them in that sickly green light was almost overpowering. With a deep gulp, he forced a rush of air into his lungs.

Before he could speak, Cleo bolted past him and out the door, her limp almost undetectable. Frank was sure he was seeing an illusion and not Jumper's ghost. He also knew that anyone clever enough to pull off such a hoax could be a real threat.

Without turning his back on the image, he stepped outside the RV. Cleo was standing behind a tree, peeking around its trunk, her eyes wide as she stared at him.

Frank motioned to her to stay put and then crept around the RV to the back. He carefuly scanned the woods but saw no one. Coming back to the RV, he peered into a window at the back. The telltale wires of a stunt harness hung in the dim green light inside. Held in the harness was the figure of the ghost.

Frank flipped open the doors of several compartments in the outside wall of the RV until he finally found the fuse box. "I thought so," he muttered as he saw that a fuse was missing. A small box holding spares was attached to the door of the box. He got out a new fuse and screwed it in. Instantly light shone through the windows.

Cleo, encouraged by seeing the light from inside the RV, came out from behind the tree. "Stay here," Frank urged. "Let me take a look inside first."

Cautiously, Frank stepped back inside the RV. The lights were bright enough to show that the main room of the vehicle was empty. Frank made a quick, careful search of the other rooms and closets and found no one.

Then he turned his attention to the "ghost." He discovered a cable strung along the ceiling of the RV. The harness was rigged to travel along the cable. "Remote control," he said softly, as he noticed the telltale tiny red light.

Hanging from the harness was one of Jumper's

costumes, stuffed with plastic foam. Sitting on the shoulders was a molded head of Jumper Herman. "A great illusion," Frank said aloud. "I wonder what Cleo would have done if I hadn't been there."

Using a rag from the kitchen to protect the rigging from his fingerprints, he carefully removed the harness from the dummy's body. Then he laid the body across the dining table. He stuffed the harness and the cable rigging into a paper bag he found in a cupboard. Then he carried the whole illusion outside and explained it to Cleo.

"That's the artist's model they use in the makeup trailer," Cleo said. "I've seen it there. I can't believe this. The ghost seemed so real."

"It was definitely done by a pro," Frank agreed. "I'm going to return the costume and head."

"I'll go with you," Cleo said. "I'm not ready to go back in that RV yet."

Frank piled the Jumper dummy and the paper bag into the back of the golf cart. Cleo held the head in her lap as Frank drove them to the wardrobe trailer.

The wardrobe mistress was surprised when Frank turned over the Jumper costume. "So, someone's been playing games, hmmm?" the costumer said, removing the foam filling from the Jumper costume. "There's way too much weirdness around for me."

"So this is the Bigfoot costume," Frank said, pushing the hangers aside to get a better look. "How did you do your research on this?"

"The usual," the woman said. "You'd be surprised how many books and articles there are on the subject. We also talked to some of the locals before we made our final costumes."

"Cool," Frank said. "Anyone from Crosscrook?"

"Have you met Sassy Leigh?" she asked. "She's working on the film as a story consultant—a real expert on the folklore of this area. She was a lot of help."

"Yes, I met her," Frank said, lifting the feet of the Bigfoot costume. "Wow, look at these," he said, continuing his interrogation. "How big are these feet?"

"Well, the legend says the feet are supposed to be up to twenty-five inches long by about ten inches wide," the costumer answered. "And we made the first pair of feet to those dimensions. The actor who plays Bigfoot is pretty tall, but he said he felt like he was wearing clown shoes, so we made this pair smaller. They work great."

"They've got tread on them like running shoes," Frank observed.

"Yeah," the costumer said. "He's gotta move pretty fast across that mountain."

These sure aren't as big as those prints I saw outside the abandoned cabin, Frank thought. And mine didn't have any tread marks. He rubbed the hair of the costume between his fingers. This doesn't feel like those clumps I found, either.

Next, Cleo led Frank to the makeup trailer. Frank carried the head inside and was greeted with a round of cheers.

"Thank you, thank you," one of the makeup artists cried, cradling the head in her arm. "We thought we'd have to make another one. We use this for reference when we make up Berk, and sometimes they use it for stunts. Where did you find it?"

"It was on top of a dummy dressed in a Jumper costume, Hilda," Cleo answered quickly. "Someone tried to pull a practical joke."

"If they only knew how much time and effort it takes to make one of these models," Hilda said with a sigh.

"You have no idea who might have taken it?" Frank asked, looking around.

"No," Hilda answered. "People are in and out of here all the time. We have studio security, but no one's actually posted outside the trailer. I mean, who would expect someone to come halfway up a mountain to steal a tube of lipstick."

"So you think it might be an inside job," Frank said. "Someone involved in the production."

"No way," Cleo said. "Who?"

"I don't mean that exactly," Hilda said. "I'm just

wondering who from the outside would want it."

"And want it enough to come all the way up here to get it," Frank agreed.

He walked around the trailer, checking out the wigs, false mustaches and beards, and other cosmetic tricks. "You've got everything here," he observed. Everything someone would need to create a perfect disguise, he added to himself.

"Show him what you showed me the other day," Cleo urged Hilda. "Make me a redhead—ten years younger and ten pounds lighter."

"I'd love to see what you can do," Frank said.

The makeup artist sat in front of a computer and took Frank through a complete program of graphically enhanced design.

She started by bringing up an image of Cleo's face, which was already stored in the computer. Then, using the computer drawing software, she changed the hair color and style, the eye color and the shape of the nose. She could even make Cleo look like a man by adding a beard and mustache. Finally Hilda made the Cleo image look younger and thinner.

Frank was familiar with the computer drawing software, but he had never used it to change a real person's appearance. "It is totally amazing," he agreed. "Thanks for showing me how it works.

Cleo, I'm going to check the shooting schedule, and then get some lunch."

"Are you in the press conference scene, by any chance?" Hilda asked.

"Yes," Frank answered.

"Postponed till tomorrow," Hilda said, without turning around. At Cleo's urging, she was turning the young star's computer image into a green-eyed blond woman.

"Then I'm turning in my costume and heading for some food now," Frank declared.

"You go ahead," Cleo said, her eyes still on the computer screen. "I'm having way too much fun to eat." She seemed to have forgotten her panic at seeing Jumper's ghost.

Frank took the paper bag with the harness and rigging from the ghost illusion to the truck and stashed it in the locked compartment after turning his costume in and changing into street clothes.

As he walked away, he felt a whoosh of breeze as someone raced past him. Experience made Frank mentally record the man as he passed—tall, dark tan complexion, black mustache. A navy backpack with red straps bobbed against the man's shoulders as he ran.

As Frank logged the description in his mind, he heard a voice calling from his left. "Stop him! Grab that guy!"

Frank turned long enough to see that the man yelling for help was a studio security officer. That was all he needed. He ran after the man with the backpack for about ten yards. Then with an effort worthy of an Olympic athlete, Frank lunged forward and tackled his quarry.

8 A Startling Attack

Frank's flying tackle landed with a solid hit. He and the man slammed to the ground with a gut-grinding thud.

The stranger was strong, but Frank wrestled him on to his side and held him down. He could hear the security guard approaching. Then, in an instant, his hold was broken. The man he'd tackled caught Frank in a leg hold and flipped him over. Frank twisted to grab again, but the stranger wriggled free and disappeared into the forest.

Frank got to his feet and followed, running beside the security guard. As they approached the edge of the forest, they heard a motorcycle start up ahead of them. In seconds the sound of the zooming motor faded away until it was a faint hum in the distance.

"We lost him," the security guard said. He turned to Frank. "Thanks for the try. You almost had him."

Frank identified himself as one of the film's crew and gave the guard a description of the man with the backpack.

"I thought I recognized you," the guard said. "You're one of the animal wranglers, right?"

"Right," Frank said. "Who was this guy, do you know?"

"Not sure," the guard said as they walked back to the set. "One of the guys in editing called. Says he saw this guy sneaking around. He called him on it, and the man had no ID. He could be somebody we've been watching for—a real troublemaker."

"Who?" Frank asked.

"Now, you don't have to worry about that," the guard replied. "You just keep those beasts of yours under control, and I'll take care of the trespassers. But thanks again for your help."

The guard smiled, but Frank could tell from the man's expression that their conversation was over. Frank nodded his head and said, "Okay, see you around."

"Yep," the guard replied. He started to walk away but then turned back. "Say, you know that stunt guy Lavring, don't you?" he asked Frank.

"Yes—why?" Frank asked.

"I hear he's still hanging around the area—staying in town somewhere," the guard said. "If you see him, tell him he'd better stay away. The studio means business on this one."

"I'll tell him," Frank said. In fact, I think I'll go tell him right now, he thought as the guard walked away.

"So you're still here, Terry," Frank muttered to himself. "I don't know what your part is in all this, but I'm going to find out. There must be *some* reason why you haven't left."

While Frank was driving into Crosscook to find Terry, Joe was around the mountain on the other side of the shooting location. He, Gene, and Lloyd were working with Omar, rehearsing Omar's big scene. A delay had changed the shooting schedule, and it was still a couple of hours before their scene.

The set was of the plane crash. The wreckage looked as if the plane had nosed right into the side of the mountain. At the far edge of a clearing, an abandoned cabin sat just inside the forest.

"Okay," Gene said as Lloyd eased Omar out of the trailer. "I know we've gone over today's scene a dozen times, but one more time won't hurt. Joe, you stand in for Berk; I want to be sure we've got this cold."

74

Joe nodded and mentally went over the scene in his head, picturing every move he'd make.

Omar twitched his ears and sniffed the air. "Easy . . . good boy," Lloyd murmured, patting the lion's tawny head. "You hear something, do you? It's okay." Joe knew from his training that Omar sometimes needed the reassurance of his trainer's voice to calm him.

As Lloyd spoke, Omar lifted his head, and Joe could see him relax. The animal leaned against Joe's leg and then sank to the ground to lie down. His back legs sprawled to one side, but his front legs stretched out in front, and his head was straight and alert. He reminded Joe of the Sphinx.

"Today's scene starts with a 'long shot showing the tail of the plane jammed into the mountain,' " Gene recited, reading from the script. " 'Jumper emerges from the forest and moves to the wreckage of the plane.' "

Gene checked his script before continuing. " 'It's been a long hard search,' " he read. " 'Jumper's dirty, caked with blood, and woozy from hunger and thirst. He combs the area around the site of the crash, frantically searching for the missing bag. He finally limps toward the cabin.' "

Joe followed Gene's gaze to the small building. He recognized it as a model of the abandoned shack Terry had taken them to see. It was a replica of the cabin that supposedly was Jumper's hideout.

As Gene talked through the scene, Lloyd held Omar's leash loosely in his hand. Joe got the cooler of small pieces of raw chicken that would serve as Omar's food rewards during the shoot. He stuffed a plastic bag with several hunks in it into his jacket pocket.

" 'As Jumper is looking for the bag,' " Gene concluded, reading from the script, " 'Omar stalks him. At first he remains hidden, weaving in and out of the trees. Then he becomes more aggressive, growling and threatening. Finally, he crouches and leaps toward Jumper. Jumper is startled, then terrified. Omar brings him down in a terrifying wrestling match.' "

"Then we switch Jumpers," Joe remembered.

"Right," Lloyd said. "I'll be the stunt double for Berk during the wrestling scene."

"We may not even get that far today," Gene pointed out. "Dustin may want to shoot that scene separately, without a lot of onlookers."

"Yeah, it'll be more like playtime at home," Lloyd said, giving Omar a friendly pat. "Right, pal?"

They ran through the scene a couple of times, then stopped. Omar was acting restless. "Looks like he knows his big scene is coming up," Joe said, grinning at Gene. The golden tan puma paced back and forth. Slowly curling his tail from side to side, he strained at the leash Lloyd held.

"I'm going to take Omar back to the trailer for some water and a rest," Gene said. "The crew won't be arriving for half an hour. I want to talk to the cameraman, too, to make sure he knows what to do if Omar gets distracted."

"Great," Lloyd said, handing Gene the leash. "When you see Dustin arrive, just take Omar into the woods and wait for the cue."

"Sounds good," Gene said, walking Omar off.

Joe was beginning to feel pumped. It was Omar's biggest scene in the movie, and his job was to make sure the mountain lion had plenty of treats to make him comfortable.

"I wonder where Frank is," Joe said. "He thought he'd be here for the shoot."

"He said he was going to sign on as an extra," Lloyd said. "He might show up later."

"Could be," Joe said, looking around. "He was also going to do some investigating. Maybe he's on the trail of a good lead."

Gradually the film crew began showing up, and at last Dustin arrived. As soon as he settled into his director's chair, everyone quieted down and got ready to work.

"Okay, now, everybody, you all know the scene," Dustin said. "Berk," he called to the star, "are you with us?"

"I'm coming, I'm coming." Berk walked onto the set, and applause rippled through the cast and crew. The transformation of the actor into the character was amazing.

"Wranglers, are you ready?" Dustin asked. "Is our stand-in here?"

"Ready," Lloyd answered. Joe walked to the mark Lloyd pointed out to him. Joe looked into the distant woods. The puma's golden tan face peeked out between the trees.

"Okay, once with the stand-in," Dustin called out. "Then we'll try it with Berk."

"Listen up, everyone," Gene said. "Omar is a safe animal, as safe as a mountain lion can be, but he's still a lion and a wild animal. The first rule is this: whatever happens, don't run. If you run, you become prey."

Joe heard a murmur of anxiety ripple through the crew.

"If there's a problem, don't run," Lloyd repeated. "Just stand still and then do whatever we tell you. Our number-one goal is your safety. This is a difficult scene. Omar will be unleashed briefly. When he's off the leash, there's a chance he'll get curious and wander off the path. I repeat once more—if that happens, don't move. We'll take care of it."

When he finished his announcement, Lloyd took his place at the edge of the set.

Dustin nodded at Joe. "Let's do it," he said.

While Dustin walked Joe through the scene, the

crew took light readings and adjusted camera settings. Finally the moment came for Omar's appearance. "Okay, wrangler, it's time for the cat," Dustin called out.

At that moment Joe's back was to the film crew. He was facing Lloyd. The puma would sneak up behind Joe, moving toward Lloyd.

"Come on, let's go, fellows." Dustin's voice sounded behind Joe.

Then he heard Lloyd call out from the edge of the set. "Gene! Let him loose! We're . . . Okay, there he is. Omar just stepped out of the woods, Joe."

Joe felt a rush. In his mind's eye, he pictured Omar stalking toward him.

Lloyd's voice pierced the image in Joe's mind. "Hold it, everyone," the wrangler said.

Something about the change of tone in Lloyd's voice made Joe catch his breath. He heard a gasp from behind him, and then another. He turned slowly. The puma was walking toward him. Even though he knew it was a just an act, Joe still felt a spark of adrenaline shoot through his body.

"Joe, stop," Lloyd murmured. "Don't move. That's not Omar."

Lloyd's words sliced through the air. The puma paused and gazed at the wrangler. Then the sleek head turned back, its eyes focused on Joe. The puma's head was raised into the air, its chest billowing as it caught a scent. Then it hunched its head down into its shoulders. Staring steadily at Joe, it stalked toward him.

It was very quiet, and Joe felt drops of sweat break out on his temples.

"What's happening, Lloyd?" Dustin asked in a low voice. "What's going on?"

"Don't anyone move," Lloyd repeated. "I'm right behind you, Joe. I've got the tranquilizer gun. Do not raise your arms. I'm going to knock the cat out. Everyone stand very still."

Even though Lloyd stood nearby, his voice seemed so far away to Joe. It was almost like an echo. Joe took small breaths, barely moving his chest. His body told him to run, but his mind knew he had to follow Lloyd's command.

The mountain lion stopped abruptly. Then, with a low rumbling growl, it pounced in a graceful arc aimed sraight for Joe.

Joe was trapped. The puma was in the air, leaping toward him. Lloyd was standing behind him, about to shoot the tranquilizer dart. If Joe moved, he'd be shot. If he stood still, he was lion lunch.

9 Where's Omar?

Joe stood transfixed, watching the puma fly through the air toward him.

"Now, Joe!" Lloyd called from behind. "Roll!"

Joe heard the *ping* of the tranquilizer dart gun firing. Remembering his training, he dropped to the ground, kicked out his feet, and rolled to one side.

Surprised by the dart's sting in its flank, the pouncing puma twisted and missed a direct hit on Joe. It bounced off Joe's legs and thudded to the ground.

Joe jumped to his feet. He could hear Lloyd's voice in his mind as he remembered the first day of training. "If you're threatened by a mountain lion," Lloyd had said, "try to make yourself look as big as possible. Open your coat out to make the puma think you're wider."

As Lloyd had taught him, Joe took the corners of his open jacket and held them out wide like huge wings. Never taking his eyes off the lion, he slowly backed away.

The puma tried to rise to launch another attack on Joe, but its legs were wobbly, and it fell once more to the ground. This time it stayed.

"Everyone back away," Lloyd said, "and leave the area." No one needed to hear that order twice. The set was cleared in just a minute.

"Man, that was close," Lloyd said as he lay his head on the puma's chest to double-check its heartbeat. Then he touched the puma's left ear. "This is how I knew it wasn't Omar." Joe looked at the edge of the ear. There was a piece missing, as if something had bitten out a small hunk.

"It's a good thing—" Lloyd started to say.

"Lloyd, Omar is missing," Gene interrupted, racing onto the set. "When I went to pick him up for the scene, he and his cage were missing. I turned to yell at you and someone punched me."

"Are you all right?" Joe asked.

"Yeah, it was a body blow right to the gut," Gene said. "It took all my wind. By the time I could get back here, it was too late. This puma was leaping straight at you, Joe."

"And the chicken in your pocket," Lloyd pointed

out. "That's probably what attracted him." He stood up as he spoke. "We've got to get this cat locked up for now and then find Omar!"

"The trained animal's missing, and a wild animal shows up for the shoot," Joe said. "Way too much coincidence. Someone had to set the whole thing into motion—just another way to disrupt the filming."

"But this time it was dangerous and could have been deadly," Gene pointed out. "Although this couldn't be an entirely wild puma," he added.

"What do you mean?" Joe asked.

"A really wild puma would never wander into an area with people standing around," Gene said while Lloyd checked the lion's pulse and examined its eyes. He wanted to make sure it wasn't having a bad reaction to the tranquilizer.

"He would have stayed hidden or run away," Lloyd added.

"Are you saying it's someone's pet?" Joe asked.

"Not necessarily a pet," Gene said. "But it's definitely used to being around people or it never would have walked out here in the first place."

Joe, Lloyd, and Gene dragged the tranquilized cat to the wranglers' trailer. The animal was heavy, but they finally managed to secure it in one of the cages. Lloyd put a pan of water in the cage and locked the trailer.

"We've got to find Omar!" Lloyd said. Joe could

83

hear the worry in his voice. "Who knows where he's been taken."

"I'm worried about Gus now, too," Gene said. "What if they've gone to the compound and taken him? We've got to get back there."

"Look, if the catnapping was just a prank, they might let Omar loose," Joe said. "What would he do? Where would he go?"

"He won't run away," Gene said.

"He'll try to follow our scent or the scent of his trailer," Lloyd said. "If we drive back to the compound, that's where he'll go if he can."

"So it's not necessary for one of you to stay here in case he comes back?" Joe asked.

"Not if we move the trailer down the mountain," Lloyd answered.

"All his feed is in the barn down there, too," Gene pointed out. "That will also be a draw. I'll check in with Dustin, and then let's go," he said, running off toward Dustin's RV.

Lloyd showed Joe the part of the mountain forest where the puma had made its entrance. The two explored the woods, but found only a red bandanna, which Joe stuffed into his jacket pocket.

Joe and Lloyd also checked the area around the trailer very carefully. But they didn't find anything that might tell them who had taken Omar.

The sun had warmed the mountainside, and Joe peeled off his jacket. One pocket held the red bandanna he'd found in the woods. He pulled the still-cool chicken pieces out of the other pocket and returned them to the cooler. Then he threw the jacket into the wrangler truck and locked the door.

"Wait a minute, there's only one truck here," Joe said. "Did one of you drive the other one someplace else today?"

"No," Lloyd answered. "Why?"

"Well, if none of us drove it away, it was either stolen along with Omar, or Frank's taken it somewhere." He combed his hand through his hair and looked around. He saw people rehearsing, repairing sets, adjusting cameras, talking and eating, but no Frank.

"I've got to find Frank," Joe told Lloyd. "He should be around here somewhere. I also want to talk to studio security to see if they saw anything funny."

"Good idea," Lloyd said. "We'll take the trailer and see you back at the compound."

"You go straight back and check on Gus," Joe said. "Frank and I will stop in town and report the catnapping—and maybe a truck theft—to the Crosscook sheriff."

Gene rejoined them, saying that Dustin had revised the shooting schedule. The wranglers were free to search for Omar.

"We're out of here," Gene said, sprinting toward the trailer. "We'll see you at the houses."

Joe watched the wranglers drive off and then headed to the security trailer.

"Joe!" Sassy called from behind. "Wait! I have to talk to you."

"I'm in a big hurry, Sassy," Joe said, turning.

"Well, I heard what happened on the set," she said. "Are you all right?"

"You'd make a good reporter," Joe said, smiling. "Nothing happens around here that you don't find out about—almost immediately."

"Hey, that's my job—folklore, remember?" Sassy pointed out. "I have to be on top of all the rumors and tales and find out which are true and which aren't. So is your story true? A wild puma stalked you while you stood in for Berk?"

"That's pretty much it," Joe said. "You didn't see what happened?"

"No," Sassy replied, obviously disappointed. "But everyone's talking about it. So now we need to find out whether the mountain lion was sent to do damage or was just after the food in your pocket."

"You've got quite a network, Sassy," Joe said. "Come to think of it, you can be a real help to me right now."

"Wonderful," Sassy said, taking out her purple clipboard. "What's my assignment?"

"Tell me where Frank is," Joe said. "I've lost track of him. Have you seen him?"

Sassy seemed disappointed that she wasn't getting a real investigator's task. "I saw him drive the truck away about an hour ago. I don't know where he was going. He did have a scuffle with someone earlier, though."

"He what?" Joe said. "What are you talking about?"

Sassy told Joe what she'd heard about Frank and the man with the blue backpack.

"Do you know who it was?" Joe asked.

"I heard it might have been a guy who wrote a book about Jake Herman," Sassy answered. "But I don't know for sure."

"And you haven't seen Frank since he drove off?" Joe asked.

"Sure haven't," Sassy said. "Just one more mystery to solve. This is the best film I've ever been on," she added, her green eyes wide and round. "It's absolutely wonderful." Her rust-colored eyebrows arched high as she smiled.

"Well, I'd better get going," Joe said. "Are you going to be around the set all day? I might want to talk to you later."

"Sure," Sassy replied, with a small salute. "Look me up anytime."

Joe went to the security trailer and talked to a couple of guards. Neither had seen anything suspicious leading up to the puma's attack.

One of the guards was the one who had been

with Frank earlier when the backpacker escaped on the motorcycle. "I'll tell you the same thing I told your brother," the guard said. "If you see your friend Terry Lavring, tell him he'd better not get caught hanging around these sets."

Joe was surprised by the guard's words but smiled and said, "If I see him, I'll tell him."

As Joe walked back to the truck, he decided to follow Frank's trail into town. I have to report the theft of Omar to the sheriff, he reasoned. Maybe I'll see Frank in town someplace and I can pick him up then.

As Joe approached his truck, his keen eyes saw immediately that something was wrong. Although the door was shut nearly tight, it didn't quite line up with the rest of the truck. A small dent in the edge of the door told Joe what had happened.

He barely touched the handle, and the door swung open. It was a little crooked, not enough to attract a lot of attention. It hung at such a weird angle, though, that Joe knew the locked door had been pried open.

A scribbled note was impaled on the turn signal lever: "Back off—or there'll be no escape the next time."

Joe reached for his jacket, heaped on the floor. This time both pockets were empty. The red bandanna was gone.

10 Crisis in Crosscook

"Okay," Joe muttered. He looked at the empty pocket of his jacket where the red bandanna had been. "This is getting personal now."

"There he is." Joe heard Dustin's distinctive British accent. The director and Berk were heading Joe's way. Berk still wore his costume.

"Berk tells me you and your brother were with Terry Lavring when he was informed of his firing," Dustin said to Joe.

"That's right," Joe said.

"Did he make any threats?" Dustin asked.

"No," Joe answered. "What's this all about?"

"We heard Lavring is still in the area," Dustin said. "Then today we saw someone else prowling around the editing trailer. We're wondering if the two might be working together to cause trouble."

"That puma attack was pretty scary," Berk added. "I've been thinking all along that the problems we've had during the filming were just pranks, but this latest thing—that could have been *me* out there. *I* could have been attacked by the wild puma."

"Exactly," Dustin said. "The so-called gags have escalated into real danger. And my stars are under attack. First Cleo, then Berk. If Lavring is behind this, I won't rest till he's behind bars."

"Just let us know if you see him," Berk added.

Dustin nodded and the two walked off.

Joe jumped into the truck and pulled the door closed. It wouldn't latch completely, so he got a hunk of rope from the metal supply chest and tied it closed.

Then he headed to Crosscook to find Frank.

When Frank had pulled into Crosscook a couple of hours earlier, he was determined to find Terry. It didn't take long. Terry's sleek red sports car was parked on the main street. Frank guided his truck into a parking place nearby and went inside a small restaurant.

"Frank," Terry called out when he saw Frank. "Great to see you. Join me for something."

Terry was sitting in a booth along the back of the

restaurant. He was dressed in a red nylon windsuit with a silver streak down the arms and legs.

"I thought you'd been banished from the king-dom," Frank said, taking a seat at Terry's table. He told Terry about the security guard's warning.

"Hey, they can ban me from the set," Terry said, "but they can't keep me out of Tennessee! I have a nice suite at the inn across the street. I'm not leav-ing town until I find out who sabotaged my stunt. I've checked my stunt rigging, and it was definitely tampered with."

The waitress brought Terry a burger, fries, and soda. Frank looked over the menu and ordered the same.

"So what's happening with Cleo?" Terry asked, dousing his fries with ketchup. "Is she back on the set? I miss working with her. I haven't seen her since the hospital. She's got a lot of courage—she'd make a great stuntwoman."

Frank told Terry about the script being rewrit-ten to account for the young star's sprained ankle. But he stopped short before telling the stunt mas-ter about the ghost illusion he'd seen in Cleo's RV that morning. He was quiet for a minute, thinking of the rigging he'd taken from Cleo's ceiling that was locked in his truck.

Finally he turned to Terry. "Do you ever set up any of your stunts for a prank?" he asked. "Or to pull a practical joke on someone?"

"Sure," Terry admitted with a grin. "What's the fun of knowing how to do all this stuff if you can't fool your friends once in a while?"

Frank took a bite of his hamburger. He was surprised to realize how hungry he was. He hadn't had anything to eat since his light breakfast—and that seemed like a long time ago. He thought about the ghost illusion in Cleo's RV. Terry definitely could have pulled that off, he told himself. But why?

"Have you seen a motorcycle around town this morning?" Frank asked. "With a tall man toting a blue backpack?"

"No," Terry answered. "Why all the questions? How come I feel like I'm getting the third degree?"

Frank told him about the man he had tackled.

"Well, I don't know who it was," Terry said, piling more mustard on his hamburger. "Have you and Joe figured out who's been targeting the production?" he asked. "You've got to tell me everything you find out."

Terry took a big juicy bite of his sandwich. He stared off into space as he chewed. Then he looked back at Frank with an intense stare. "I need all the evidence I can get," he said. "I'm thinking about suing the studio."

Frank heard the door open behind him. "And speaking of suing the studio," Terry said, with a sweeping arm gesture. "Look who just walked in. Ernesto, join us. I thought I saw you coming into the inn last night."

Frank turned to see a tall man enter the room. He was dressed in black jeans and a black turtleneck. The man smiled and waved at Terry, but his expression turned cold when he saw Frank.

"It's motorcycle man," Frank muttered to Terry.

"I'll join you only if you can confirm that your friend here isn't going to wrestle me to the ground," the stranger said.

"Hands off, I promise," Frank said. "Actually, I'd like to hear your story." The man seated himself across the table from Frank.

"Frank Hardy, Ernesto Roland," Terry said. "Ernesto wrote *Parachute to Peril, the* book about Jumper and his exploits."

"I've heard of the book," Frank said. "It got a lot of attention when it came out."

"Yeah," Ernesto said, waving the waitress over. "It got a lot of attention from this studio, too. So much that they lifted whole sections of it for the *Dropped into Danger* script." He ordered a bowl of soup and a ham sandwich.

"So Ernesto sued the studio," Terry explained. "He accused them of stealing from his book. He said they'd used his book for the script without paying him."

"I lost the first round," Ernesto said. "But the

appeal is filed. I'm not going to let them get away with it."

"The security guard said you were sneaking around the editing trailer this morning," Frank said. "That was you taking off on the motorcycle after you broke my hold, wasn't it?"

"No comment," Ernesto replied, glaring. His mustache twitched as he spoke. "Of course the studio doesn't want me hanging around. They don't want me to see how much of my book they're using in the script. But they're not going to keep me away. I need evidence and I'm staying until I get it."

"I'm with you, man," Terry chimed in, taking a big slug of soda.

"They're stealing my work, and I'm going to prove it," Ernesto said, grabbing his water glass. "No matter what it takes."

Anger flooded Ernesto's expression, and for a moment Frank thought he was going to throw the glass. Then his mood seemed to pass, and he took a deep breath.

Ernesto's outburst made Frank realize that the author had a real grudge against the production. Could he be responsible for the rest of the incidents? Frank wondered.

"Hey, maybe Frank and his brother can help you," Terry said. "They're detectives. I took them up to Jumper's old shack last night to snoop around a little."

"I've already been on the receiving end of Frank's work," the author said. "But I don't need any help, thanks. I prefer to work alone."

"You must have spent a lot of time up on the mountain while you were researching your book," Frank said. "You must have found some things while you were here."

"You collected a lot of stuff, didn't you?" Terry said to Ernesto. "I figure that you found lots of items that were probably Jumper's around the old shack. At least you hinted at that in your book."

"Could be," Ernesto said. "I have a few items. I wouldn't say I found them exactly. Let's just say they were given to me—a letter to Jumper from his daughter, a photo, even some things that might have been part of the loot he stole."

Frank thought Ernesto might be hedging the truth a little. He knew the author didn't dare admit that he had actually found evidence of Jumper's crime. If he did, he would have to turn it over to the police in charge of the investigation.

Frank could also tell that Ernesto was flattered by the attention he was getting and happy to brag a little about his collection.

"Do you have any of it with you?" Frank asked, hoping to draw the man out. "I'd love to see an actual Jumper Herman artifact."

"Sure, I always bring a few things when I

travel," Ernesto said. "I never know when I might run into a buyer, someone who'd like to own a little Jumper history. It pays to be prepared—to have a few samples on hand." He took a sip of soda. "We could go over to the inn when we're finished eating."

"It'll have to be some other time for me," Terry said. "I've got some business to take care of. Frank, maybe we can meet this evening. I want to talk about my stunt sabotage." Terry left so quickly that Frank didn't have a chance to answer.

"I heard about the trouble with Cleo Alexander's stunt," Ernesto said. "Terry thinks it was sabotage? That means someone was targeting Cleo. Or Terry, since it was his design. Who would do that?"

"That's what we're trying to find out," Frank said.

Frank and Ernesto finished their lunches and paid their bills. Then they walked across the street to the inn, which looked as if it had once been a large beautiful home. Ernesto led Frank up two flights to his room at the end of the hall.

"Wait," Frank said as they approached the door. The skinniest possible sliver of light was showing between the door and the jamb, and Frank knew it meant that the door wasn't closed. For a moment Ernesto held back while Frank walked cautiously toward the door.

Frank's ears strained to hear the slightest rustle,

the tiniest scrape from the other side of the door. But he heard nothing.

"This is ridiculous," Ernesto roared from behind him. "If anyone's in my room, I'll kill him!" He pushed past Frank and shoved the door open.

11 Who Growls There?

Ernesto pushed the door so hard that it slammed back against the wall. The sound echoed down the hall.

The sight of the chaos in the room took all the bluster out of Ernesto. He seemed to become paralyzed, leaning against the doorjamb, unable to take the step across the threshold.

The bathroom door at the far end of the room was open, but there was no sign of anyone, so Frank cautiously stepped inside.

The rooms had been totally ransacked by someone apparently in a big hurry. No effort was made to conceal the fact that someone had been there. Drawers were left in a jumbled pile. The mattress was still half on the boxspring, half on the floor.

Suitcases lay open, clothes and hangers were heaped on the floor.

One of the windows was open. When Frank peered out, he saw a roof five feet below the window sloping down to an alley. A perfect escape route, he thought.

As Ernesto walked around the room, he was unexpectedly calm. "Can you tell if anything is missing?" Frank asked.

Ernesto turned slowly to Frank. He seemed lost in his thoughts. It was almost as if he'd forgotten Frank was there. Finally he spoke. "I told you I prefer to work alone," he said. "Leave now, and don't tell anyone what's happened here. I'll report it in my own time."

"But—"

"You heard me," Ernesto said. "Get out."

Frank backed out of the room, stepping over the litter on the floor. As he was leaving, Ernesto began to pick up drawers and insert them into the dresser.

Frank walked down the stairs to the lobby of the inn. His mind felt almost as jumbled as Ernesto's room as he thought over all the strange occurrences since he had left the compound that morning. "I've got to find Joe," he muttered. "He'll never believe what's been happening."

"Well, look who's here," Sassy Leigh called out as Frank walked across the small lobby. "Have you been visiting one of the guests at the inn? I understand Terry Lavring is still in town. Cleo said she had a midnight snack with him last night after she was discharged from the hospital."

"Hello, Sassy," Frank said. "I could ask you the same question."

"Actually, I heard that Ernesto Roland is also lurking around town." She reached into a large black tote bag and took out her purple clipboard. "He's always been one of my heroes. I was hoping to get his autograph." She leaned in as if to tell Frank a secret. "Frankly, I agree with him. The film's scriptwriters borrowed more than a little from his book. If I were Ernesto, I'd be angry, too."

"So far the courts don't agree with you," Frank pointed out.

"Yes, but the latest appeal may bring a different verdict," she answered. "How's your brother doing? That was quite a scare!"

Frank's attention focused quickly, every sense alert. "What are you talking about?"

"Why, the mountain lion attack, of course," Sassy answered. "Don't tell me you don't know about it."

"Omar attacked Joe?" Frank asked.

"Omar is the trained puma's name, right?" Sassy said. "Well, apparently it wasn't Omar. It was a wild animal that just wandered onto the set."

"Was Joe hurt?" Frank asked.

"No, he's fine," she assured him, and told him what happened. "But apparently, your actor lion was taken, so the wranglers are pretty upset."

"Sassy, you'll have to excuse me," Frank said. "I've got to get back to the compound right away."

Frank sprinted out of the inn and back across the street to the truck. In minutes he was headed to the studio compound at the edge of town. He skidded to a stop in front of the wranglers' house and ran inside.

"Frank!" Joe said, clasping his brother's shoulder. "I looked for you in town and saw your truck. But everywhere I went, like the diner, they said you'd just left. I decided to come back here to wait. I knew we'd have to hook up sooner or later."

"I'll tell you all about everything later. I want to hear about your run-in with a wild puma. How are you?"

"Still here," Joe said with a lopsided smile. "Thanks to good training and Lloyd's tranquilizer dart."

"We've been out looking for Omar," Gene said as he and Lloyd came in. "He was taken from the trailer, but no luck finding him. We came back, hoping he'd wander back here, too."

"I talked to security," Joe reported. "They saw nothing strange. Trucks and equipment go up and down the mountain all day. If someone can flash an ID, that's all they need," Joe said. "I also talked to the Crosscook sheriff. He's going to get some of the locals together to launch a search. He promised to let us know if anyone spots Omar."

"Yeah, but I want to find him before they do," Lloyd said. "I'm sure the sheriff means well, but they will still be treating Omar like a wild animal. We've got to get to him first."

"Do you have any kind of a plan?" Frank asked. "Any ideas about where to look?"

"We've already spent time searching the edge of the town and all through the woods behind the compound," Gene reported.

"Now we want to go up the mountain to about halfway between the location site and here," Lloyd added. "Park the trucks and head out on foot. If Omar was released anywhere in that area, he should be following the scent back here. Maybe we can pick him up along that trail."

"We know it's a long shot," Gene said. "He could be clear out of Tennessee by now . . . or worse. But we have to try. He'll respond to our voices, so we've got to give it a shot."

"I think we ought to take both trucks," Lloyd said. "Then if we need to split up, we can. You two follow us."

"Let's go," Frank said. The trucks were always packed with rescue, survival, and capture equipment, so they just jumped in and headed out.

While Joe drove the second truck, Frank told him about his day. He described the ghost sighting in Cleo's RV, reaching back to show him the harness and rigging that had been used for the illusion.

"You know," Joe said, "that's something Terry could have cooked up if he hadn't been sent away."

"But he didn't go," Frank said, and told Joe about finding the stunt master in town. "Sassy said something weird, too," Frank remembered. "She said Cleo told her she'd had a late snack with Terry last night."

"So, they're pretty good friends," Joe pointed out.

"But Terry said he hadn't seen her since last evening in the hospital," Frank said. Then he told Joe about the special effects makeup and the costumes—especially Bigfoot's.

"What are you saying?" Joe asked. "How does that figure into all this?"

"I'm not convinced that I was shoved by a bear yesterday," Frank answered.

"You think it might have been somebody wearing the Bigfoot costume?"

"Possibly. Several people have mentioned seeing him . . . it."

"Whatever," Joe said with a chuckle.

"It could be part of a plan to terrify everyone—

or someone—involved with this movie," Frank concluded.

"But who?" Joe wondered. "And why?"

"I met a prime candidate today," Frank said. He told Joe about tackling Ernesto and then eating lunch with him, and the mess they found later in his room.

"You're right," Joe said. "He definitely moves to the top three or four."

"Who else are you thinking?"

"I hate to say it, but I keep coming back to Terry," Joe said. "I know the wranglers think he's clean, but there's something that keeps pointing to him."

"But why would he do it—what's his motive?" Frank wondered. "Well, I'm glad he stayed around. We definitely need to talk to him some more. He wants to talk to us about the failed stunt. We can get more information then. He's got a reputation for being a little hotheaded. Maybe there's been bad blood between Dustin and him."

"Right," Joe agreed. "So that's four suspects—Terry and Ernesto Roland . . ."

"And?"

"Bigfoot and the ghost of Jumper, of course!" Joe said, giving his brother a mock surprised look.

"Sassy is definitely hoping it's one of them," Frank said. "We need to talk to her more, too. She's the best source for what's going on behind the scenes. She's the one who told me about you and the wild puma. She's like a pipeline up and down the mountain."

"Looks like we're stopping here," Joe said, following Gene's lead and slowing the truck. It was three-twenty.

The four decided to stay together, at least for the first part of the search. They armed themselves with packs full of flashlights, ropes, animal collars and harnesses, scraps of meat, water bottles, and knives and other forest survival items. Gene and Lloyd carried tranquilizer guns.

They were determined, but it seemed like an impossible quest. The area was wild and unspoiled. If Omar were out there somewhere, he was certainly not alone. Many creatures could be watching them, stalking them, or slithering around them.

It was so dark deep in the woods that the searchers lost their sense of time and place. "What was that?" Joe whispered. From the corner of his eye, he thought he saw a shadowy form moving from tree to tree or ducking behind a boulder. "Must have been a tree limb," he answered himself as they moved on.

They had walked about fifty yards when a familiar smell wafted past Frank's nose. He followed the acrid odor to the left through some tangled undergrowth. Then he lost the scent. "Did you smell that?" he asked the others in a low voice. There was no response. He looked around but saw no one. In an instant, he realized he had wandered off the trail they'd been carving through the forest.

Carefully, Frank retraced his steps through the undergrowth. A strange sound behind him made him pause for a moment to listen. It was a low throaty warbling sound. It was like a warning, a nervous noise broadcasting imminent danger. White-hot waves rippled up Frank's back and seemed to explode in his temples.

He took another cautious step forward. The sound behind him changed to a long gutteral growl.

Frank turned around slowly and took a step backward. He puckered his dry lips and managed a shrill whistling sound, one that he knew would get Joe's attention.

He still couldn't see what was hiding in the undergrowth in front of him, what was threatening him with that low rumbly growl.

Frank took one more step backward and felt his foot sink. The ground disappeared completely beneath his foot, and he plunged down into a dank black pit. Above him, snarling and flashing its ferocious fangs was the softly wedged face of a mountain lion.

12 A Cabin of Clues

Frank's piercing whistle cut through the dense forest. "That's Frank," Joe said when he heard it. He looked around. "It came from back there."

Joe led Gene and Lloyd back in the direction of Frank's whistle. "Whoa, look at that!" Joe said, spotting the mountain lion standing in the path in front of them. Its long tail flashed back and forth, and a red bandanna was tied around its neck. A small hunk was missing from the edge of its left ear.

"Stand still," Lloyd reminded them all. "It's been around people." He drew his tranquilizer gun, just in case, but it wasn't needed. The cat bolted away.

"I'm down here," Frank called when he heard their voices.

Joe and Gene rushed to the edge of the pit. "I'm going after that cat," Lloyd said. "It's the same one that attacked you this morning, Joe. You three follow me when you get Frank out."

"Hey, are you okay?" Joe flashed his beam around the bottom of the pit. Frank was standing, smiling up at him.

"I'll tell you what——I'd rather see your face up there than the one that was looking down at me a few minutes ago."

"Let's get you out of there," Joe said. "Are there any toeholds—anything you can use to climb up?"

"No, I've already checked," Frank answered. "This was some kind of well, I think, but the stones that lined it crumble when I touch them. We'll have to use ropes."

Joe and Gene tied their ropes together and lowered them to Frank. The two of them anchored the lifeline as Frank climbed to the surface. Back on firm ground, he unloaded his vest pocket.

"I found these at the bottom of the well," he said. "They were buried pretty deep, but the ground is so soft down there—nothing but mud and weeds. I stirred things up when I landed." Joe flashed his light beam on the objects in Frank's hand.

"Looks like pieces of a belt or strapping for something," Joe said, picking up the two strips of leather.

"And this is silver, I think," Frank said, holding up a chain. "It's corroded, but it might clean up."

"Where's Lloyd?" Frank asked, putting the objects back in his pocket. "And what happened to the lion?"

"They both went thataway," Joe said, gesturing to the right. "I suggest we do the same."

"Agreed," Frank said. "But I want to come back here tomorrow when it's lighter to look around."

Joe, Frank, and Gene followed the path beaten through the forest by Lloyd chasing the mountain lion. The thick brush and undergrowth began to thin out after about forty yards, and they caught up with Lloyd at the edge of a small clearing.

"Shhh," Lloyd warned them. "Look at that." Joe, Frank, and Gene stopped and followed Lloyd's gaze.

In the glow of twilight they saw a small cabin. Although old, it appeared neat and cared for. Leading away from the far side was a narrow dirt road with tire-tread marks. "Looks like someone lives here," Joe said in a low voice.

"At least a four-legged someone," Lloyd pointed out.

Walking across the clearing was the mountain lion with the red bandanna around its neck. When it reached the cabin, it gave the front door a nudge and sauntered inside.

Joe, Frank, Gene, and Lloyd crossed the clearing and peered through a window. They were look-ing in on the main room of a two-room cabin. They could see through a doorway into a large kitchen at the back.

The puma was lying on the top tier of a bunk bed in the corner of the main room. Totally at ease, it licked its paw, then rubbed it across its face. There was no sign of a human resident.

Joe went to the front door, which was ajar. Care-fully, he inched it open, Frank, Gene, and Lloyd right behind him.

At first the puma stopped washing its face and stared at the trespassers. Its tail swept back and forth, indicating its annoyance at being disturbed. Its ears flattened against its head, and its lip curled up a little to show sharp fangs.

Joe talked to it the way he'd been taught to speak to Omar. "Easy, boy," he said. "It's okay. Easy . . . easy. Gooooood boy."

Joe stared at the cat but didn't move. Finally the puma's ears relaxed. In another minute it resumed its face-washing.

Never taking his eyes off the puma, Joe stepped inside the cabin. The cat watched Joe and the oth-ers enter. Although its tail kept up its flipping and flopping, it sighed and seemed to tentatively accept their presence.

"I'll keep an eye on him—and the front door," Gene said. "You three look around." He leaned against the wall, and he and the puma settled into a stare-off.

"Coffee," Frank said, sniffing the aroma curling out from the kitchen.

"And a fire," Gene said as the telltale sounds crackled through the air.

"Someone definitely lives here," Joe said, "and probably isn't going to be gone long."

"Such a tiny clearing in the middle of this enormous mountain forest," Lloyd pointed out. "We'd never have found this place if we hadn't followed the puma."

"I grew up here," Gene said from his sentry post. "There are thousands of cabins like this that no one knows about tucked into mountainsides. The lion is obviously a pet and pretty trusting. It was probably raised as a kitten, with little experience as a wild animal."

"I'm sure this is the lion that wandered on to the set this morning," Lloyd said.

"And that's probably the bandanna I found," Joe said, "the one that was stolen from the truck."

"You told us that puma had to have been brought to the set, right?" Frank asked the wranglers. "You told us wild pumas are very shy. It wouldn't have just walked into a group of people."

"That's right," Gene said.

"And whoever planted him there must be someone who really knows the area," Frank pointed out. "Someone who knows how to manage the puma and steer it on to the set."

"Like the owner of this cabin," Joe said. "Let's find out who that is."

Joe, Frank, and Lloyd poked around for a few minutes. At first they found nothing important. The cabin had only a few pieces of furniture, and there weren't many personal items lying around.

"Hey, what's this?" Joe said at last. He was standing next to an old wooden door propped up against the corner of the room. He pulled the door away and leaned it against one wall.

"Easy, boy, easy," Gene murmured to the lion, who perked up its ears. It looked intently at Gene for a few minutes, then rolled onto its side and closed its eyes.

"Look at this," Joe said. Moving the old door had revealed a beat-up trunk tucked into the corner. Joe eagerly hoisted up the lid. Inside was a surprising treasure. Clothes, wigs, mustaches and beards, eyeglasses, stage makeup, canes and other accessories—everything a person would need to turn himself into many different people.

"Hello," Frank said, digging deep into the trunk and pulling out a hairy Bigfoot costume. "Guess what this is supposed to be." He looked it over carefully, then concluded, "This is different from the movie costume."

"It's in a lot worse shape," Joe observed. He

pointed out a few rips and one place where the fur had completely worn off.

"Whoa, what's that?" Gene whispered, from his spot against the front wall.

"What's the matter?" Lloyd asked, his voice low. As he spoke, the puma rolled up to his feet and stood on the top bunk. He stared at the front door.

"I thought I heard something coming up that road out back," Gene said.

"Let's get out of here," Joe warned. "Looks like Daddy's coming home."

Frank stuffed the Bigfoot costume back into the trunk. Joe shut the lid and slid the old door back in front of the trunk. Quickly, they darted back out the front door.

Joe's feet and his heartbeat seemed to race in rhythm as he led the others back across the clearing toward the woods. But he stopped cold when he heard the scratchy warning voice: "Don't turn around or you'll be dinner for my roommate!"

13 Unmasked

Joe, Frank, and the wranglers stood very still when they heard the threatening voice behind them. Joe wanted to turn around, but he didn't know whether the person was armed.

"Now, you all don't want to be turnin' around," the person said as if reading Joe's mind. "You don't need to see who I am or what I'm holding in my hands, aimed in your direction."

"That roommate you're talking about," Joe said. "Would that be the puma we saw in the cabin?"

"It would," the person said. "His name is Elvis. Only he's not in the cabin anymore. He's standing here. And he's eager to do a replay of this morning's scene. All he needs is my signal."

"Hey, it was a great stunt this morning," Joe

said. "I really thought Elvis was a wild animal. I'd sure like to meet his trainer. How about it?"

"Nice try," the person said with a nasty chuckle.

"Do you have our puma?" Lloyd asked. "Did you take Omar?"

"Well, now, I thought it best not to have two pumas on location," the person said. "So I removed yours temporarily."

"Where is he?" Lloyd asked.

"You'll get him back soon enough," the voice replied. "I'm not going to keep him. I got my hands full with Elvis. I want you trespassers off my property. Don't turn around. Don't look back. Just get out of here. If I ever catch you here again, you'll become a permanent part of the Smokies."

"Okay, we hear you," Joe said, taking a deep breath. "Come on, guys, let's go." Frank, Gene, and Lloyd followed Joe out of the clearing and back into the forest.

From behind a tree, Joe took one quick look back. He wasn't close enough to see the person clearly. But he rattled off a few things to the others as they ran by. "Medium height," he whispered, "long shaggy hair and beard, big shotgun."

It took the four a while to retrace their steps and get back to their trucks. "It's getting so dark," Lloyd said. "I'm going to check in with the sheriff on the way back. I don't trust that guy back there.

I want to see if the sheriff's search has turned up anything on Omar."

"Good idea," Gene said. "I'll go back with the Hardys. I need to check on Gus."

Joe watched Lloyd drive off, then pulled the other truck onto the road. "So who was that guy, I wonder," he said as he drove. "And why did he disrupt the film shoot?"

"There was something about his voice," Frank said. "I think I've heard that voice before."

"Do we know for sure it *was* a guy?" Joe asked. "I couldn't tell by the voice, could you?"

"No, but you said he had a beard," Gene said.

"And a trunk full of disguises," Joe reminded them. "So who knows?"

It was nearly seven o'clock by the time they pulled into the compound. Gene went straight to Gus's trailer to check on the bear. Joe went to the barn to get some feed for Gus. An odd sound from up in the loft caught his attention.

Armed with a pitchfork, he climbed the wooden ladder to the loft. When he saw the large camel-colored form, he dropped the pitchfork and yelled. "Frank! Gene! Get in here—quick!"

Joe scrambled up the rest of the ladder and hurried to Omar, lying in the straw. His feet were tied, and he seemed to be very woozy.

"What is it, Joe?" Gene called from below.

"It's Omar! He looks like he's been drugged."

Gene climbed the ladder, two rungs at a time. After a quick examination, he guessed that Omar had been tranquilized. He and Joe untied Omar's feet and Gene rubbed the big cat's legs.

Slowly, Omar seemed to get his bearings. He sat up once but fell back. Then he sat up again and shook his head. This time, he kept his balance.

Gene nuzzled Omar and murmured to him. The immediate sound of a chain-saw purr made the wrangler laugh out loud.

Rather than try to wrestle the cat down the ladder, Gene decided to leave him in the loft until he had the strength to get down by himself. Frank and Joe piled up bales of hay to give Omar a larger stair step approach to the floor of the barn. Gene decided to stay with Omar until the cat was back to normal.

Frank waited at the house for Lloyd to return so he could tell him the good news about Omar. Joe went down to pick up dinner for the four of them.

By the time they finally fell into their beds, the Hardys agreed they'd had a full day's work. "In all the commotion, I forgot to ask you something," Joe said, turning out the light next to his bed. "Did you tell Terry about the ghost of Jumper in Cleo's trailer? Did you ask him if he had anything to do with the illusion—maybe as a joke?"

"I wanted to, but something held me back," Frank answered. "If Terry set up that trick to scare

Cleo, he might be behind some of the other incidents around here. I want to get more evidence before I say anything to him. If I tip my hand too soon, he'll know we suspect him."

The soft patter of rain on the roof helped quiet Joe's racing thoughts as he finally slipped into sleep.

Wednesday morning Joe was awakened by rain pounding on the metal roof and a knock at the door. When he opened it, he saw only a cardboard box addressed to Frank. Joe took it back to their bedroom and awakened his brother.

"No return address," Frank mumbled as he looked at the box. No postage or delivery stamp either," Joe pointed out. "It must have been delivered by a courier of some kind."

Frank cut open the box. He pulled out the newspaper used for packing to reveal a navy blue backpack. He opened the bag and spilled out several videotapes. Each was marked with a date and a label, such as "Jumper cabin," "plane," or "press conf."

"Ernesto's backpack," Frank said.

"Looks like he's been shooting a few scenes himself," Joe said, "with a video camera. That must be why he was hanging around. Why'd he send them to you?"

"Terry told him that we're investigating the trouble with the film. Maybe he thought these would help."

"Hey, guys, you up?" Gene called. "I've got breakfast."

Gene unloaded the breakfast burritos and eggs he'd picked up at the commissary. He told the Hardys that filming would be suspended until the afternoon, when the rain was supposed to stop. Then they would be shooting scenes at the Jumper cabin location. Frank showed him the backpack and tapes.

"I told Dustin that Omar's back," Gene added. "He wants to meet with Lloyd and me this afternoon to reschedule his scenes. You guys will be free until tomorrow."

"Great!" Frank said. "I want to go back to that old well I was chased into. I'm thinking that those leather strips and silver chain might have something to do with Jumper. I'd like to see if we can find anything else."

"Be careful," Gene warned. "Whoever it was that caught us at that cabin last night seemed pretty dangerous. I don't want anything happening to my new wranglers. At least not until the filming is done," he added with a goofy smile.

Lloyd came in from checking the animals. Shaking water from the wide brim of his leather safari hat, he reported that Omar had suffered a bout of nausea during the night. But now their prize puma had fully recovered and was sleeping it off in his trailer.

Over breakfast, the four wranglers talked about the package of tapes Frank had received. "We need to take a look at them as soon as possible," Frank said.

"This is a different size tape than our camera viewer plays," Gene said. "But I think Terry's videocamera takes this size—and he's got an editing viewer, too. He uses it to check his stunts. We ought to be able to play this tape on one or the other. I'll call him."

Gene was back from the phone in just a few minutes. "He says to come over. He wants to see the tapes, too. And I videotaped the rehearsal yesterday morning while Joe was standing in for Berk. We can take a look at that also."

"Great," Joe said. "We can view the tapes before we head out to the woods this afternoon."

Again, the four wranglers took both trucks, the Hardys in one and Gene and Lloyd in the other. That way they could leave Terry's and go on to their afternoon destinations without returning to the compound.

Terry had a large suite at the inn, with a sitting room separate from the bedroom. He already had the editing viewer and his videocamera viewer ready when the wranglers arrived.

The Hardys, Gene, and Lloyd told Terry about their search for Omar. The stuntman seemed intrigued by the cabin full of disguises and the strange man and his pet puma.

Finally they all got to work. "This is so cool," Terry said, popping the first tape into his camera viewer. "Maybe I can find out who messed up my stunt."

All five huddled around the table and watched the tape on the small built-in window in the viewer.

"Can we boost the volume?" Gene asked.

"No, that's as high as it goes," Terry said.

"Don't forget, Ernesto probably was hiding when he shot these videos," Frank reminded them. "It's a wonder we have any sound at all."

"What are we looking for exactly?" Lloyd asked.

"Any evidence that might show who took Omar, for one thing," Gene answered.

"Or who planted Elvis to take Omar's place," added Joe.

"Or who tampered with my rigging," Terry said.

Frank focused on the small screen. Finally, after half an hour of viewing, something clicked. "Wait a minute," he said. "Go back a little."

Terry rewound the tape and played it again.

"There!" Frank said. "See that guy—the one in the red shirt?" The shot showed the man from the side. He was nearly bald, with a fringe of pale hair. A large scar emerged from under wraparound sunglasses and snaked down his cheek. "I talked to him yesterday. I didn't get his name, but he's one of the extras."

"And?" Terry asked.

"Last night I thought I recognized the voice of the person who chased us away from his cabin," Frank said. "That's the guy," he said, pointing to the man in the viewing window. "The person at the cabin sounded like this extra."

Frank turned to Joe. "Did the cabin guy walk while you watched him?" Frank asked. "This extra has a limp."

"I didn't see him move," Joe said. "But he was standing sort of lopsided, now that you mention it. He was leaning over to one side, like maybe one leg is shorter than the other."

Terry popped the tape into his editing viewer and printed a still shot of the video where Frank had asked him to stop the tape. He handed Frank the photo of the extra in the red shirt.

After they finished viewing Ernesto's tapes, Lloyd slipped his tape from Joe's stand-in rehearsal into the editing viewer.

"What's that?" Joe asked as they watched. Terry paused the tape, and Joe pointed to a bulky shadow near a large tree. The shadow was a long sleek form next to a rounder bulge. Terry cut and printed that shot and scanned both prints into his laptop computer.

Terry's photo-viewing software allowed him to enlarge the views, lighten the tones, and sharpen the images. With Frank's guidance, he worked on the two photos. It took a while, but when they were through, there was no doubt about what they saw.

Terry called up both shots, side by side. The image on the right showed the actor in his costume as an extra in the film's cast.

The image on the left was the same man, only this time, he had shaggy hair and a beard and was crouching near a large tree. His arm was resting on the back of Elvis, the puma that had attacked Joe, and his hand was clutching the fold at the nape of Elvis's tan neck.

14 The Illusion
Crumbles

"It's the same man," Terry said. Frank studied the two images. The man who had unleashed the puma on Joe and the man who'd caught them trespassing was the man he'd talked to—an extra in the movie. All three were the same man.

"Let's go," Frank said. "It looks like we've had a break in this case at last. We need to get more evidence before we go to the police, though. Let's see if we can find this man at the filming location. I also want to see if I can find Ernesto in town and have him look at the strips of leather and silver chain I found in the well. He's the ranking expert around here on Jumper Herman artifacts. He might be able to authenticate them for us."

"The rain has let up, so they're probably thinking about shooting at the cabin after lunch," Lloyd pointed out.

"I could try to find Ernesto for you," Terry said. "Maybe set up a meeting for later."

"Good idea," Joe said, looking at his watch. "It's ten-thirty now. Frank and I will be at the food tent on the mountain between one and one-thirty."

"Lloyd and I should be through with our meeting with Dustin by then," Gene said. "We'll meet you there."

"One of you call me here about then," Terry said. "I'll try to get Ernesto lined up."

"It's a plan," Joe said. He and Frank took Ernesto's videotapes and the two enhanced photos and left.

On the way to the location, Frank and Joe talked about the events of the last two days and how they could possibly be related.

"If the guy in the photos is really responsible for Elvis's attack on me," Joe suggested, "he could be behind *all* the weird stuff that's been going on. He's got those costumes and disguises in that trunk in the cabin. Even the shaggy beard and hair could be fake, for all we know. He could use all those disguises so it would be hard to trace the crimes and pranks to just one person."

"He had a Bigfoot costume in the trunk, too," Frank said. "He could have been the one that knocked me down Monday. He even could have been spying on us through the window of the abandoned shack that Terry took us to on the way to the hospital. He could be the one behind *all* the Bigfoot sightings around here."

"What about Cleo's stunt?" Joe wondered.

"Was it an accident? Or was it intentional? And if so, who set it up—and why? Terry swears someone sabotaged his rig, but he also swears he didn't leave it long enough for anyone to tamper with it. He can't have it both ways."

"You're right—his story doesn't add up," Frank said. "But I really don't think he's behind this stuff. We'll talk to him about it this afternoon."

As soon as Joe parked the truck, Sassy raced over to greet them. "Have you heard?" she said breathlessly. "Ernesto Roland has been arrested!"

Sassy rattled on almost nonstop about how Ernesto had been caught lurking around the set again. "But this time he was caught and taken to the county jail in a town a few miles from Crosscook," she said.

She turned to Frank, and her green eyes narrowed. "Remember when we ran into each other yesterday at the inn?"

Frank nodded, and Sassy continued. "Well, when Ernesto went back to his room at the inn— practically at the same moment we were talking— somebody had completely ransacked it. You were in the area then. Did you see anything funny?"

"No, but I have a question, and I can't imagine anyone better to ask. You know everything that's going on around here."

Sassy's eyebrows rose when she heard Frank's words. She leaned forward and said, "I certainly try to know everything. How can I help?"

"It's about one of the extras. He looks familiar to me—an old family friend, maybe. But I can't remember his name. He's got really shaggy hair and a shaggy beard—"

"Hank Jeamer," Sassy interrupted. "I'm sure that's who you mean. He's a local and kind of a character. A real loner. He's not down here every day—just shows up occasionally. He lives up in the mountains. And he looks the part so perfectly that Dustin always signs him up as an extra when he does show up."

"Yep, that's him," Frank said. "I told Joe—if anyone would know, it would be you. Thanks a lot."

"Sassy, I've got a question for you," Joe said. "What if I found something that looked like it might have a connection with Jumper Herman. My first impulse would be to have Ernesto Roland take a look at it. But it sounds like he might be out of commission for a while. Is there anyone else around here that could authenticate an item?"

"You're looking at her," Sassy said, shrugging her shoulders.

"Of course," Joe said.

127

"I've collected some pretty interesting things myself," Sassy said. "Have you found something? Tell me about it. Tell me everything." She pulled her purple clipboard from the huge black bag hanging from her shoulder.

"No, no," Joe said, holding up his hands. "I don't have anything yet, but I'll let you know."

"Well, when that happens . . ." Sassy wrote a few lines on a piece of paper. "Be sure I'm the first to know." She handed Joe the paper with her address and telephone number written on it.

The Hardys started to move away, and Sassy called after them. "By the way, I haven't seen Hank today, but if I do, I'll tell him you're looking for him."

"No, don't do that," Frank said quickly. "I want to surprise him. Let's keep it our secret."

Before she walked away, Sassy nodded and put a finger in front of her mouth, indicating that she would keep quiet.

"I have an idea," Frank said. "Come on." He led Joe over to the makeup trailer. Frank reminded the makeup artist, Hilda, that he had been there before with Cleo. "I wanted to show my brother that cool software you have that alters facial images," he said.

"No problem," Hilda said. "The program's always open. Just don't mess with any of my files. I'm going to pick up some lunch. Lock up if you leave before I get back. Everyone's kind of nervous, what with all the peculiar incidents around here."

As soon as Hilda left, Frank scanned in the photo of the shaggy-haired extra. Then he used the computer to "erase" the big beard and shaggy hair.

"So now we have a clean palette," Joe said, staring at the picture. All they saw was a bald head shape, eyes, and a nose. Frank added a fringe of pale hair and a jagged scar down the cheek. "Yes!" he said. "It's the man I talked to yesterday. They could definitely be the same person in two disguises."

Frank stared at the name he'd written on the bottom of the photo: Hank Jeamer. In the distance, he saw another photograph hanging on the wall.

Joe followed his gaze. "Are you thinking what I'm thinking? Whoa, could it possibly be?" He darted across the room and took down the photo of Jumper Herman. Frank scanned Jumper's image into the computer. Then he told the computer to age the image twenty-five years. It was the balding Hank Jeamer with the fringe of hair. Frank drew a scar on the cheek and the transformation was complete.

The shaggy-haired Hank Jeamer and the balding man with the scar and Jumper Herman could all be the same man!

Frank looked over at Joe, who was rapidly jotting letters on a notepad. "It's an anagram," Joe said, showing the notes to Frank. "If you scramble *Hank Jeamer* you get *Jake Herman*—Jumper's real name!"

Frank and Joe looked at the three faces on the computer screen, then at the anagram puzzle Joe had solved. "Jumper!" Joe said. "Still alive!"

"Still taking chances," Frank added. "Still fooling everyone, still taunting the authorities."

"An extra on the movie about himself," Joe said. "It's perfect. From everything we've heard, it's exactly something this guy would do."

Frank printed the images he had concocted. Then he deleted all the work he had done in the computer. Joe hung the photo of Jumper Herman back on the wall and then headed out to meet Gene and Lloyd for lunch.

The wranglers were waiting for them. They had been dismissed for the day and were eager to go up the mountain to look for clues. Over sandwiches, the Hardys shared their suspicions with the wranglers. Gene and Lloyd were excited by the possibility that Jumper was alive and hanging out on the set of *Dropped into Danger*. They all agreed that they should go back up to the cabin where the puma had led them the night before—perhaps the cabin where the famous Jumper Herman now lived.

"Let's stop by Terry's first," Frank said as the four piled into one of the wrangler trucks. "I want to ask him about the ghost illusion in Cleo's trailer."

The inn was quiet. It was midday, and no one was in the lobby except a lone desk clerk reading a magazine. Frank led the others up the stairway and down the hall to Terry's room.

As they neared the door, they heard voices shouting. Frank turned to the others and held up his hand, urging the others to be still.

"I swear I haven't told anyone," they heard Terry say from the other side of the door. "I promised I'd keep it a secret and I will. So stop bugging me about it."

"I can't help it," the other voice wailed. "Nothing kills a career faster than being branded as trouble on a film. If anyone finds out we planned the whole thing, I'll never work again."

Frank's jaw dropped as he heard the second person speak. The voice was unmistakably that of Cleo Alexander.

15 You're Too Late

"I mean it," Frank heard Cleo say from behind Terry's door. "I trusted you with this whole scheme. If you rat me out, I'll never forgive you. If I go down, you go with me."

"Relax, Cleo," Terry said, his voice lower. Frank and Gene leaned toward the door. "No one's going to find out."

The conversation stopped. Frank waited a minute, then knocked on the door.

Terry opened the door. His face was flushed as red as his T-shirt. Frank wondered whether that was because of anger or embarrassment at seeing the group at the door.

"Well, look who's here," Terry said. "You guys should have called first. I'd have ordered up some snacks or something." He stood in the doorway, not budging.

"We've been out here for a few minutes," Joe told him.

"Ernesto was arrested," Terry said, not responding to Joe's statement. "I tried to set something up for us with him. He's out on bail now, and he'd be happy to look at the things you found in the well if you're still interested."

"We'll talk about Ernesto later," Frank said. "Look, Terry, we know Cleo's in there. We heard you shouting at each other."

"Well, come on in then," Terry said with a sweeping gesture of his arm. "Join the party."

Cleo was sitting on the sofa in front of the large bay window. She wore a yellow jumpsuit and her Olympic windbreaker. "Hi, fellas," she said with a small smile. "I guess if I want to keep a secret, I need to learn to keep my mouth shut."

"We came over because we have a lot to tell you, Terry," Joe said. "But first we need some answers. And you've got to be straight with us."

Terry frowned at Cleo, then turned back to the wranglers and gave them a crooked smile. "I think I know where you're going with this. Go ahead—ask."

"Where were you yesterday morning?" Frank asked.

Terry sighed and uttered one word: "Busted."

"I'm dead," Cleo said. "My career is over."

"Terry!" Gene said. "Are you saying—"

"Cleo's RV . . . the ghost of Jumper floating down the hall," Terry said, nodding his head. "A pretty good illusion, considering the small space I had to work with."

"But how could you do that to Cleo?" Lloyd asked. "You know how nervous she's been with all the threats and everything."

"Get real, man. It was *her* idea," Terry said.

"He's telling the truth," Cleo said with a sigh.

"I was tired of everybody laughing at me when I told them someone that looked like Jumper was hanging around," she said. "I talked Terry into creating the illusion."

"Then she invited you there, Frank, so you could be a witness," Terry said. "Neither one of us counted on you being such a great detective. It took you just a few minutes to figure the whole thing out. I've been waiting for you to ask me about it."

"What about the problems with her flying stunt?" Joe asked. "Did you two plot that, too?"

"Absolutely not," Terry said firmly. His dark eyes flashed with anger. "Someone sabotaged that stunt—it could have been a disaster. And I'm not leaving until I find out who did it."

"Okay, I believe you," Frank said. The others nodded in agreement. "And we might just have a suspect for you."

The Hardys and the wranglers all talked at once, telling Terry and Cleo what they'd discovered.

"Whoa, this is huge," Cleo said. "You have to take me up to that cabin with you. If I can help solve this, I'll have enough publicity to carry me for a year."

"Look, we can't all go," Frank said. "We'll scare him off."

"Well, you're not leaving me out," Terry said. "I'd even offer my car, but it won't seat us all."

"We can take my studio car," Cleo offered. "It's a luxury sedan. Plenty of room. But I go, too."

"What'd I tell you," Terry said. "She's got the guts of a stuntwoman."

"It's probably a good idea not to take one of the wrangler trucks," Frank said. "If Jumper, or Hank, or whoever it is spotted it, he'd know immediately who was coming."

There was no way the wranglers could leave Terry or Cleo behind, so they all climbed into the young star's sleek car and started up the mountain, with Terry driving.

Joe's navigation skills were so attuned that he steered Terry onto the old road that they had seen leading away from the back of the cabin. There were no other vehicles around, but they parked about twenty yards from the cabin, just in case.

They grabbed cables and ropes from Terry's

trunk. Gene and Lloyd were armed with their tranquilizer guns. Joe led them up the road.

The smell of wood smoke hung in the air, but there was none coming from the chimney. It was about three-thirty, and the sun suddenly shot from around a cloud for the first time that day. The clearing around the cabin was suddenly painted with light and shadows chasing back and forth.

When they reached the cabin, Joe paused for a moment, listening for any sound from inside the building. He heard nothing. His senses on high alert, he quickened his pace and headed toward the front window. The others followed closely behind.

Joe crouched beneath the window, then slowly raised his head and peered inside. Elvis was lolling on his high-bunk perch, lapping his paw. There was no sign of the cabin's owner.

Joe turned to the others to report what he'd seen. Something fluttering in his side vision captured his attention. "Uh-oh," he said when he spied the piece of paper tacked to the front door. "Come on, Frank," he said. "The rest of you stay here." Gene and Lloyd pulled out their tranquilizer guns, just in case.

Joe and Frank crept to the door. With a feeling of total letdown, Joe yanked the paper off the door and read the message aloud: " 'You're Too Late.' "

When he pulled off the paper, the cabin door creaked open. Elvis looked up for a moment, but then went back to his bath. "The disguises are gone," Joe said, seeing the empty corner where the trunk of costumes and accessories had been.

"Except for that one," Frank pointed out.

The Bigfoot costume was draped as if it were sitting in the chair. On its lap was a letter from Jumper Herman. Joe sank down to a stool and read the letter:

" 'Gentlemen, I've finally overstayed my welcome in this glorious part of the world,' " Joe read. " 'You two hotshots are about to blow my cover and I'm bugging out before that happens. After my plane crashed a quarter of a century ago, I lost part of my treasure. I have been here since, gathering up the missing items. Although the movie was a flattering idea, it was also an enormous imposition. It increased the risk that others would find my missing treasure before I did.' "

In the letter Jumper went on to say that he did his best to discourage the project by disguising himself as himself in his younger days and appearing as a "ghost."

"He could really pull that off," Frank said. "As the extra cast member Hank Jeamer, he had complete access to the sets and locations."

" 'I substituted my mountain lion, Elvis, for

yours and took your splendid puma,' " Joe read on.
" 'Of course, I had to case the wranglers' house
and barn area Monday night in preparation for the
catnapping. I apologize for knocking out the young
wrangler in the process.' " Frank rubbed the back
of his head as he remembered the blow he had
received.

Jumper went on to assure the reader that Omar
had been well cared for because he loved pumas
and would never endanger one. He also said that
he followed the Hardys and Terry when they
checked out his original shack.

"He must have been the driver of the car that
barreled out in front of us," Terry said.

In the letter Jumper mentioned Frank, Joe,
Gene, Lloyd, and Terry by name. He also said that
the Bigfoot costume was well-worn because he
had used it decades ago to scare off townspeople
and tourists from his property.

" 'I haven't used it in the last ten years,' " Joe
read, " 'since I scared a group of developers who
wanted to build vacation condos nearby. Whoever
finds it is welcome to it.' "

Finally Jumper said that he didn't know where
he was going and couldn't risk taking Elvis. He
asked that Gene and Lloyd make the cat a permanent resident of their animal care facility.

Gene, Lloyd, Terry, and Cleo were exhilarated
to be part of the mystery solving. "Man, I can't

wait to tell everyone," Gene said. "This is cool."

"They'll have to reinstate me," Terry proclaimed. "This letter is proof that Jumper's been causing all the trouble on the production."

"I can see the headlines now," Cleo said. "I'd better schedule a press conference for tomorrow."

"To think that we almost caught the famous Jumper Herman," Lloyd added.

"*Almost* caught," Joe repeated, slumping down on the stool.

Frank knew how Joe felt. They had come so close to cracking this case before Jumper left. If only they had figured it out a little sooner, they might have been able to catch him.

"Terry, can you drive Gene to the compound so he can get the truck and a cage for Elvis?" Lloyd asked. "I'll stay to make friends with him."

"Fine," Terry said. "How about the rest of you?" he asked, turning to Frank. "You coming?"

"I'd still like to take another look at that well," Frank said. "We've got some good daylight left."

"I'll come with you," Cleo said.

After Terry and Gene left, Frank, Joe, and Cleo headed through the forest to the abandoned well. They searched the area for nearly forty-five minutes but found nothing more. When they heard the wranglers' truck in the distance, they headed back for the cabin.

The Hardys and Terry helped Gene and Lloyd

wrangle Elvis into the cage and then strap the cage onto the truck. Lloyd gave the cat a mild sedative so that he wouldn't be anxious about being taken from his home by strangers. But Elvis seemed to have accepted his fate and settled down for the ride.

Before they left, Frank went inside the cabin and gathered up the Bigfoot costume.

The wranglers left in the truck, and the Hardys and Cleo rode with Terry. It was getting dark quickly, as it always did in the mountains. When the sun fell behind a peak, it seemed as if night arrived instantly.

Terry dropped Cleo and her car off at the Crosscook home she was using for the duration of the filming. Then, even though he was still banned from studio property, Terry felt confident enough to risk driving into the residence compound, which wasn't guarded. He drove his car behind the wranglers' house and parked.

Gene and Lloyd had beaten them down the mountain. They were at their truck parked over by the animal trailers, talking to Elvis. "Joe, can you give us a hand here?" Gene called.

As Joe walked off to help the wranglers move Elvis into his new temporary home, Frank and Terry walked to the house and stepped inside. Even in the dark, Frank could feel that something was wrong. When he switched on the light, he knew it.

It was like a movie flashback to the scene in Ernesto's room at the inn. Frank looked around. His skin crawled as if a dozen snakes slithered up his back. The inside of the house was completely trashed.

16 It's a Wrap

Frank's breath caught in quick spurts. He felt as if he had played this part the day before. Terry ran to tell the others what they'd found.

Frank called the studio security office. Then he picked his way carefully through the mess, trying not to disturb any evidence, but also looking for clues. Joe and the others came in after finally getting Elvis settled.

"You do think it was Jumper who did this, don't you?" Lloyd asked the Hardys. "Sort of a final bit of craziness before he left town?"

Frank and Joe exchanged glances. "There always has to be a motive," Frank said. "I just can't figure out why Jumper would trash this house."

"Or Ernesto's room at the inn," Joe added.

"Look, guys," Terry said. "The man's a nut. He always has been. Living with a puma on top of a mountain for twenty-five years has only made him crazier. I'm not sure we're going to find a reason that makes sense."

When the sheriff and studio guard arrived, Frank and Joe followed them around to be sure that they also saw all the evidence the law enforcement officers found.

A few fingerprints were gathered, but no one was optimistic that they would be matched. It didn't look like a professional job, done by someone who might have prints on file.

"It doesn't seem to fit the pattern of someone looking for valuables," the sheriff commented. "I wouldn't expect you fellows to have a lot of jewelry or money lying around, right?"

"The wild animals alone would scare most burglars off," the studio guard said, nervously glancing out the window at the animal trailers.

"This reminds me of an incident that we had at the inn yesterday," the sheriff said, "but we don't have a clue yet who did that job. Do you have any hunches about who's been here?" he asked Frank. "You know anybody who might want to make this mess just for fun?"

Joe handed the sheriff the letter they had found in Jumper Herman's cabin. "You might want to have a handwriting expert verify this, but I'm pretty sure it's authentic."

Frank told both officers how they had discovered that Hank Jeamer was actually Jumper Herman. Both the sheriff and the security guard were clearly impressed by the Hardys' conclusions and left to check the prints against Jumper's.

After the sheriff and guard left, everyone pitched in to clean up the mess.

"I still think it had to be Jumper," Gene said. "He was sore because you had blown his cover."

"Don't forget Ernesto's ransacking," Frank said. "The two jobs were so similar, but why would Jumper trash Ernesto's room?"

"Maybe to find the artifacts and relics," Joe reasoned. "After all, it was Jumper's loot. Ernesto's pretty open about his collection. Jumper could easily have heard about it."

Joe stopped to think for a minute. "No, that doesn't add up because how would he know *we* might have a few pieces? It has to be someone else."

"You're right, Joe," Frank agreed. "If the two break-ins are related, we have to have something in common with Ernesto. The most obvious thing is finding objects from Jumper's missing treasure."

Frank checked his locked computer case, where he had secured the leather strapping and corroded chain from the abandoned well. The lock was jimmied open, and the objects were gone. Frank and Joe looked at each other and nodded.

"Other than the people in this room, only one person knew about Ernesto's relics and also thought that we'd found some items," Frank concluded.

As he dropped the computer case onto the bed, a small neon purple triangle slipped from the handle and drifted to the floor. Joe gingerly picked it up and held it to the light.

"I'd bet anything that this is a chip from Sassy Leigh's clipboard," he said, his jaw tight.

Frank raced to the phone with the paper Sassy had given him earlier. "We've got to get her here right away," he told the others.

Frank dialed her number and asked her to meet them. "I'd like to show you some things we found this afternoon," he told her. "I'm sure they're part of the archaeological treasures that Jumper Herman stole."

Frank gave a thumbs-up to the others and then spoke to Sassy again. "We almost didn't have anything to show you after all," he said. "Someone broke into our house and really trashed it. Fortunately we had stashed the treasures in the barn out back." He was quiet, nodding his head as Sassy responded.

"Well, we're all leaving in half an hour for a meeting with one of Dustin's assistants about tomorrow's shoot. But we'll be back in a couple of hours. We could meet with you then. Great!"

"I think she took the bait," Frank reported when he hung up the phone. "She'll probably be here in about forty-five minutes, when she thinks we've left for our meeting. We have half an hour to get something set up."

The Hardys, the wranglers, and Terry began setting a trap for Sassy. Terry grabbed some equipment from his car trunk with Frank's help. Lloyd and Gene parked one of the trucks out of sight behind a building a block away. Joe grabbed the Bigfoot costume. They all gathered in the barn and went to work.

Lloyd was the lookout, and as they expected, Sassy walked up the driveway about forty-five minutes after she had talked to Frank. "Here she comes," Lloyd whispered. "She probably parked on the street so she wouldn't attract any attention."

Lloyd joined Terry and the straw-stuffed Bigfoot costume in the loft, ready to work the illusion. Joe hid in one of the stables, prepared to grab Sassy if she tried to run out the back. It was dark in the barn. Only a shaft of moonlight filtered in the dusty window across the straw, giving everything a sort of yellowish glow.

Frank was in the shadows near the front door, his senses on full alert. As he watched the door, it creaked open. Sassy crept inside and looked around. She took a few steps forward and closed the door behind her. As she stepped across the barn floor, a noise in the loft seemed to startle her.

As Sassy looked up, Frank's gaze darted back and forth from her to the loft. Sassy's eyes grew huge in the yellow light as Bigfoot himself rose up from the loft straw. He snorted a few times and lurched toward the ladder.

Sassy screamed and turned back to the door. She threw it open. Frank jumped from his hiding place to block her escape.

Sassy stumbled backward, still screaming. Gene switched on the lights. Sassy was obviously shocked to see the Hardys, the wranglers, and Terry emerge from the shadows.

"I never meant to really hurt anyone," she said, slumping to the ground.

Sassy looked out the barn window as if she were gazing far over the mountains. "It's just that . . . I found a few of the old coins two years ago. I'd been searching for years and finally found something."

She looked back at Frank and the others. "There's more out there, I know it," Sassy said, her eyes narrowing.

Then she smoothed her skirt as she continued. "I finally found what I was looking for, and then I heard that hundreds of people were coming here to spend months making a movie! Walking, driving, tearing up the place. Maybe finding the rest of Jumper's cache. I couldn't let that happen."

"So you tried to disrupt the production," Frank said.

"Of course," she answered with a bright smile. "I just needed to keep everyone away from the places I had staked out."

"You had a perfect setup," Joe said. "You got hired on as a consultant, so you had the run of the place."

"Thank you," Sassy said. "I thought it was perfect, too."

"And you wrote the notes to Cleo?" Gene asked.

"I did," Sassy confirmed.

"Did you ever dress up like Bigfoot?" Joe asked.

"Oh my, no," Sassy said. "I could never have pulled that off. But I did do anything else I could think of to get you all out of here and onto another mountain."

"Even sabotage my stunt rigging?" Terry asked.

"Mm-hmm," Sassy answered with a nod. "When your field is folklore, you learn a lot about hoaxes and gimmicks and stunts and illusions," Sassy said. "I figured out what to do so that yours wouldn't work."

"You might have gotten away with it," Frank told her. "But I have a feeling you got greedy. There was only one reason to ransack our house and Ernesto's. You were looking for treasure."

"Well, who can blame me," Sassy said. "Not only were you snooping around, trying to find out who was doing all this, you also were finding some artifacts. That was extremely unfair. I figured I was at least entitled to what you'd found. And Ernesto had plenty. He'd hardly miss what I took."

Frank called the sheriff, who arrived quickly and took Sassy away. "Before you go, I want to tell you something," Frank said. "You weren't the only person trying to make trouble. Hank Jeamer is Jumper Herman, alive and now escaped once again."

For the first time since the Hardys had met her, Sassy Leigh was speechless.

"She could be charged with attempted murder for what she did to Cleo," Terry said as the sheriff drove off with Sassy.

"Well, at least some sort of assault charge," Frank guessed.

"That'll be nothing compared to what the studio will do to her," Terry suggested. "They don't like people messing with their movies."

They all felt like celebrating but postponed it until the next day because the wranglers and Omar had early shoots.

Thursday evening the studio threw a huge celebration and party for the cast and crew. Frank and Joe were the honored guests. A planeload of pizzas were flown in from Hollywood's best restaurant.

"I have an announcement," Dustin said when he'd finally gotten the crowd to quiet down for a minute. "The studio is so thrilled with the Hardys' discovery and the worldwide publicity it is bringing that the ending of the movie will be rewritten to include the unmasking of Jumper by Frank, Joe, and their friends."

"Let's hear it for the Hardys," Berk said, leading a rousing cheer.

After the speeches and the applause, the Hardys, Gene, Lloyd, Terry, and Cleo shared enormous pizzas at a private table.

"Stuffing the Bigfoot costume and having me work it like a puppet was a brilliant idea, Frank," Terry said. "I may have to borrow it for the movie. But there's one thing that still bothers me."

"What's that?" Frank asked. He was sure he knew what the stunt master was going to say, because it was bothering him, too.

"Jumper said he hadn't used the Bigfoot costume in ten years," Terry said.

"That's right," Gene agreed.

"And Sassy said she never used a Bigfoot costume," Terry continued.

"She's too small to play Bigfoot," Cleo observed.

"So who slammed into Frank?" Terry asked in a low voice. "And who looked in on us at the abandoned shack?"

"It was a bear, of course," Frank said.

"A very smelly one," Lloyd added.

"One that ran upright on his back legs," Gene added, frowning.

"And left very Big Foot prints," Joe whispered.

BRUCE COVILLE'S

The fascinating and hilarious adventures of
the world's first purple sixth grader!

I WAS A SIXTH GRADE ALIEN

THE ATTACK OF THE TWO-INCH TEACHER

I LOST MY GRANDFATHER'S BRAIN

PEANUT BUTTER LOVERBOY

ZOMBIES OF THE SCIENCE FAIR

DON'T FRY MY VEEBLAX!

TOO MANY ALIENS

SNATCHED FROM EARTH

THERE'S AN ALIEN IN MY BACKPACK

THE REVOLT OF THE MINATURE MUTANTS

THERE'S AN ALIEN IN MY UNDERWEAR

A MINSTREL® BOOK

Published by Pocket Books

2304-06

BILL WALLACE

Award-winning author Bill Wallace brings you fun-filled
animal stories full of humor and exciting adventures.

A MINSTREL® BOOK
Published by Pocket Books

Todd Strasser's
AGAINST THE ODDS™

Shark Bite
The sailboat is sinking, and Ian just saw the
biggest shark of his life.

Grizzly Attack
They're trapped in the Alaskan wilderness
with no way out.

Buzzard's Feast
Danger in the desert!

Gator Prey
They know the gators are coming for
them...it's only a matter of time.

A MINSTREL® BOOK
Published by Pocket Books   2023